# The Candle
# of the Wicked

A HEARTH MYSTERY

# The Candle of the Wicked

## Elizabeth Brown

ZONDERVAN
PUBLISHING HOUSE
OF THE ZONDERVAN CORPORATION
GRAND RAPIDS, MICHIGAN 49506

*For there shall be no reward to the evil man; the candle of the wicked shall be put out.*

Prov. 24:20

# The Candle of the Wicked

# 1

As the Rev. Herb Tabor backed his car out of the parsonage driveway and headed in a southeasterly direction toward town he looked up, as he so often did, and took a last look at the belfry of the church. Grace Baptist, it was. Solid and dependable. Not a beautiful church, but a staunch one that had weathered many storms, meteorological and human. Just now the rays of the morning sun caught the belfry and the bronze bell that hung in it, and the bell gave off a beautiful sparkle.

Herb loved the sight of the stalwart, yet graceful belfry silhouetted against the sky. The rest of the church was not impressive, built as it was of plain, orange-colored brick with white-trimmed windows, but the belfry was distinguished. Some imagination had gone into the making of it, Herb thought as he cruised off toward Bayview. The sloping lines that ended the white portion were beautiful. The tower meant a lot to Herb. It represented something. The church had stood on that corner for nearly one hundred years and he hoped, if he stayed on at Anchorville, to celebrate the church's centennial year in a way people would never forget.

It was a hazy September morning — the tenth. School

buses were creeping along to pick up their passengers, and Herb ruefully decided, after being forced to stop several times behind the buses along the highway, that he could have chosen a better time to make his trip into Bayview. Eight-thirty caught all the later school buses. But he had promised to see two of his church members today, and the woman had said her husband had an appointment at 10:15. Herb some-what selfishly hoped there wasn't too much on their minds this fine Monday morning. He had really planned to take Evelyn and Donn for a ride along the bay, and have an end-of-the-summer picnic at one of the roadside spots. Monday was about the only time a minister's family had to get away for a few hours of relaxation. Now that Pam was in the first grade, it meant they had until 3:30 in the afternoon for themselves, to shop, loaf, sight-see, or possibly visit some friends. The rest of the week always picked up momentum, but the Tabors tried to keep Mondays for themselves.

About a mile and half from Anchorville on Bay High-way and just south of Blueberry Drive, Herb saw one of their Sunday school pupils walking along as though in a great hurry. It was Sally Ames, a fifth-grade student at one of the elementary schools on the outskirts of Bayview. She was large for her age, and looked about two years older than her ten years. Stepping along in a bright plaid miniskirt, white blouse and red sweater, Sally made a striking picture with her long, dark hair streaming in the soft wind.

She hadn't always looked like this, Herb thought as a sudden impulse caused him to slow his car and pull off to the side of the road just ahead of her. The first time he had seen her, he recalled as he waited for her to come up to the car, she had been dressed in a faded dress about two sizes too large. Her hair had been untidy and unclean, and she had looked at him with distrust, out of eyes that had been leary of trusting anyone. Sally came from a bad home environment, having a father who drank heavily, and a mother whose morals were a neighborhood byword. But the people at Grace Baptist had been able to reach into that nest of squalor and catch to themselves a jewel. In fact, Herb thought now, with some satisfaction, probably some of the church women had bought her the bright, new school outfit. Immediately he discarded the idea. Not the miniskirt, anyhow! They didn't hold with miniskirts at Grace Baptist although, of course, some of the younger ones wore them anyway. The girl was seductive, Herb thought, and doubtless did not realize it.

He opened the door of the car and called to her. "Want a lift?"

She recognized him and smiled gayly. There was no distrust in her face now, or in her eyes. They were friendly and smiling. "Oh, sure," she said, climbing into the car ungracefully. As she sat her miniskirt became a micro, and Herb shuddered inwardly.

"Boy, am I glad you came along," said Sally in her surprisingly soft voice. "I got to school early this morning and would you believe — Miss Blackport sent me home to get my geography book. I'm tired." She sighed faintly.

"That's quite a hike," agreed Herb with sympathy as he got the car in motion again. "You mean you walked all the way to school this morning, all the way back home, and now part of the way back to school?"

"That's right," said Sally with a little laugh. "I didn't mind though. It's nice out today." In a much lower voice she added, as though forgetting he was there, "and Mother wasn't home this morning, so I didn't mind."

What an awful thing to say! Tears sprang to Herb's eyes at the impact of the words. The girl hadn't minded going home *because her mother wasn't there!*

The truth of the matter was, he knew, that the girl was not the child of her mother's husband. The other children were, but not Sally. And perhaps because the girl was the product of one of her earlier indiscretions, it was reported that Mrs. Ames treated her shamefully, never tiring of humiliating her before the rest of the family and her friends. Not that Sally had many friends. The people at church had accepted her — partially at least — and a few were really concerned about the girl who had started attending their Sunday school after a Vacation Bible School program the year before. But

*11*

Sally was mainly a "loner," a youngster too old for her years, too bright and good-looking to be ignored, and not quite able to make the jump into the higher stratum of a better circle.

"Is your mother working now?" asked Herb, trying to draw the girl into conversation.

"Yes, she started last week at Dunbar's." Dunbar's was the Anchorville tavern, Herb knew, and the place where Sally's father spent most of his free time. Perhaps now Ames would choose another place, thought Herb wryly.

"You know, Mr. Tabor," said the girl suddenly, not looking at him, but at something out the window, "yesterday in church you said that God always looks after us and cares for us. I *know* He does. I know Jesus loves me because now I'm not afraid anymore when I go home. I used to be afraid every night, but not now. Not since last June."

"Well, that's wonderful to hear," said Herb, surprised and pleased. "That's the kind of news I need to make my day great. The Lord is with us indeed, in all circumstances, and there is nothing that can harm us outside His will." Ahead he saw the sign for Sandhill Drive and knew that, to take Sally all the way to her school would take him off his route, so he pulled up at the next corner, a block and a half from the school. Sally could walk that distance with no trouble, he thought. "I have to turn here," he said, and added, "We'll keep praying for you, Sally."

The girl got out. "Thank you, Mr. Tabor, I know you will," she said. She shut the car door and smiled at him through the window. "See you next Sunday!" With a flip of a hand through her long hair she turned and started off down Bay Highway, the geography book in her left hand, her right arm swinging freely at her side. Quick, young, graceful.

Herb glanced once at her swiftly retreating form as she swung off toward the school. Then he pulled around the corner and started west on Sandhill Drive. Just at the corner he met Janet Vander Cook, who was coming back to Anchorville after driving her husband Jack to work at his machine shop in Bayview. Herb waved at her and she beeped her horn. Herb felt good. He relished out-of-church contacts with his people, as the encounters at church were so formal most of the time. Seeing people only at church you didn't really get to know them, he thought. It was when you met a man on the street or in the grocery store that you really let down your hair and talked to him. He hoped some day to attain a really informal attitude with his people, but his seminary training had left him slightly stiff. Not badly so, but it was there, and he was not yet seasoned enough in the ministry to have shaken it.

When he reached the Carmichaels' place they greeted him warmly and insisted that he have late coffee with them — Donna had coffee already perked, and there were sweet rolls on the table.

"But I just ate breakfast," protested Herb half-heartedly as he allowed Donna to fill his cup, and as he took a tempting sweet roll from the plate. He wondered what they had to discuss. It had been just after the Sunday evening service when Donna Carmichael had come up to him with a strained expression on her face, and said, "Pastor Tabor, could we see you sometime at our home?"

"Of course," he had said, welcoming this open invitation. The Carmichaels hadn't been at Grace Church very long and he didn't really know them too well. He had promised to stop by the next morning.

"We have a problem," said Donna now, bluntly. "Maybe I'm wrong, and if I am you can say so, then I will try to change my attitude." She flicked a crumb off her saucer. "You know we came here just about seven months ago and have been coming to Grace Baptist. And we like it here so well; it is such a nice little town, and we have this nice home. Now," she continued with rapid-fire delivery, "having just nicely gotten settled, and making new friends, and the kids in school, Jim's firm has decided to make him manager of their plant in Detroit. This means a new move, taking the kids out of school again, looking for a new house, making new friends, finding a new church." She stopped and bit her lip. Tears came to her eyes. "I try to be a good wife," she said, "but I just can't take this moving around all the time. I love Jim and I want to do what is right. But this is the third time we've been changed, and twice in one year!"

Jim Carmichael crossed his legs and then uncrossed them again, nervously. "As far as financial gain is concerned," he said, "there isn't any question but that we'll be better off. Along with the change in position goes a $2500 per year raise. It means a big step forward for me financially. But I know it's hard on the kids and Donna. And the thing is, I can't promise that in six months or a year it won't mean moving on somewhere else."

"Well," said Herb slowly, "just what do you want me to say? Do you want me to tell you whether or not to accept the job?" While he waited for their answer he was thinking somewhat drily that he, at least, did not face a decision of a move where he would be making $2500 a year more! At least, there were some problems a minister didn't face!

"Sort of," admitted Donna, half-sadly. "Before, we just accepted the change. But this time it's different. We have really felt at home here in Anchorville, and the church. . . ." Her voice drifted off. She looked away.

"We've had a real experience with the Lord since we came here to Anchorville," finished Jim for her. "Before that we were just nominal Christians. You know. . . ." He shrugged and spread his hands. "We believed it all right, but we just hadn't really experienced it. But now the Lord is real to me, and maybe that is just my problem. I have been thinking in circles for a week, wondering if this is something He wants me to do, or a temptation that has been put in our way to test us — the promise of more money, a better house, and so on — and we have really gone over this ever since last week Thursday. I think I'm getting confused. Is it wrong to want a better job — a better house — more money?"

"I'm already confused," broke in Donna, strain in her voice. "Of course, I like the thought of having more money, too. And maybe a better wardrobe, and a bigger car — and a cottage at the lake sometime." She sat very still, and her voice dropped. "But lately I really haven't cared about these things as much. Not as much as I used to. I used to think it was great to have a brand new car. But there are so many people who don't *ever* have a new car, and they seem to be happy."

"Maybe the Lord knows He can trust you with more money," offered Herb slowly. "Maybe there is something He can do with your extra money. There is no sin in making money — it is the *love* of money that is the root of all evil, you know."

"I know that," replied Jim Carmichael. "But mightn't we come to love the money for itself? I know that if I accept this position, and do well in it, there'll likely be another raise in a year or so. I guess it is maybe moving into a different stratum of society that is scaring us."

"Well," said Herb again, thinking swiftly of several passages of Scripture that might be appropriate to use. "Jesus said: 'Take no thought for the morrow, what ye shall eat, or what ye shall wear,' but I'm sure He meant in an anxious, greedy way, not in a common sense way. He was teaching trust here, not hatred of money." He brought his New Testament out of his pocket and leafed through it to I Timothy. "Best place I know of to read is in the First Book of Timothy," he told them. "I believe it teaches attitudes, not ideas. And I've put it to good use in my own life when I get to longing after certain things I can't have." He began at the first verse of the sixth chapter and read the entire chapter.

He emphasized the words, " . . . But godliness with contentment is great gain. For we brought nothing into this world, and it is certain we can carry nothing out. And having food and raiment let us therewith be content. But they that will be rich fall into many temptations and a snare, and into many foolish and hurtful lusts, which drown men in destruction and perdition. For the love of money is the root of all evil: which while some coveted after, they have erred from the faith, and pierced themselves through with many sorrows. But thou, O man of God, flee these things; and follow after righteousness, godliness, faith, love, patience, meekness."

"I cannot tell you what you should do," he said to the couple. He sat, staring at the coffee remaining in his cup, now cold, wondering if he should be polite and drink it anyway. Reaching a decision, he drained the cup, glad there wasn't more of the cold coffee. He hoped that the Scripture he had read had been of some benefit and taken some effect. After waiting a moment he went on hesitantly.

"Each person has to be led by God in his own way. Only God knows His plan for your lives." He turned to Donna, and looking her straight in the eye, said emphatically, "The important thing is not what *you* want, but what *God* wants for you. You could stay here in Anchorville and be made to wish a thousand times you had gone to Detroit. Then, you could go to Detroit and be miserable. If God wants you here, you'll know it. He'll let you know how it is. Just pray, and wait — and listen."

"Thank you, pastor," they said almost together. "We knew you would help us. Your advice is always so practical from the pulpit, and we knew we could depend on you to give us good advice now," said Donna. "I guess we had lost sight of what really mattered. It's not what *we* want, but what *He* wants for us. Getting to know Him as we have recently makes what you just said make sense. Six months ago it wouldn't have. Now it does."

Herb rose and brushed a couple of crumbs off his sweater. It was now 9:45 and he knew that Jim had an appointment. Herb had come clad in slacks and a cardigan sweater, hoping he and Evelyn could still have their picnic. He replaced the New Testament in his pocket, and then remembered they had not prayed. "We haven't prayed," he said. They bowed their heads and he prayed simply: "Lord, show these dear people Your way for them, whether it is to stay, or go, whether Jim is to go on with his company and serve You there, or if You have something completely new — something they don't even dream of. For Christ's sake. Amen."

They were both smiling when Herb left, and, looking back, he saw that they were holding hands as they stood in the doorway waving good-by.

It was a beautiful day, he thought, sudden joy leaping inside him. He had no premonition of evil. The bay was waiting. It lay to the right of him on the return trip, a brilliant blue under the morning sky, and the air was warm already with early September warmth. The ''I don't know what in the world to wear today'' kind of weather, Evelyn would say. Too hot for woolens yet, but cooler than you liked for cottons. Herb was already perspiring in the cardigan so he took it off as he drove, one sleeve at a time, shrugging it off into the seat beside him.

His driveway. Home! ''Hey!'' he said loudly as he entered his own kitchen once again. He glanced at his watch. Ten o'clock. ''There's still time, honey. Let's go!'' Boyish, unpreacherlike, his rather square-planed face alight with anticipation, he stood in the middle of the floor grinning at his young son who was ''reading'' a large-size picture story book, the book flat on the floor before him, his chubby legs flat behind him.

''How's the boy?'' Herb asked, catching Donn up in a large swing and raising him to the ceiling. The boy squealed with pleasure.

''Do it again, daddy!'' he cried. ''Do it again!''

''You are a spoiled kid,'' said Herb as he hoisted the boy toward the ceiling again. ''A good-for-nothing, spoiled kid.'' He set Donn back on the floor and Donn promptly collapsed onto the floor in a fit of ecstatic giggles.

''Don't tell him that,'' rebuked Evelyn mildly, coming through the door into the kitchen. She was finishing buttoning the blue print blouse she had put on when she heard the car drive in. He had promised that, if the call did not take too long, they could still have the picnic. They had so few picnics. There was scarcely ever any time. Every time they planned something, it seemed, the phone rang and Herb would dash off to a sickbed, a funeral home, a family feud . . . it was endless and, sometimes on the surface, at least, unrewarding. And they needed to get away.

''I'm ready,'' she announced, looking at Herb with a

gay smile. She came closer, stood still, and wound both arms around him tightly. Her reddish hair was tied back with a ribbon in the way he liked it. Her oval face was fresh with young health. Her brown eyes sparkled.

"Don't start necking me, woman," said Herb. "Where's the food?"

"Food?" said Evelyn incredulously. "You just had breakfast and now you want food?" Dropping her arms she said to Donn, "Daddy wants food. He'd rather have food than a kiss." Donn turned to look at her soberly.

"I didn't say that," said Herb, laughing at her. She didn't fool him. He knew her well, after eight years of marriage. He knew that in the refrigerator was a well-planned picnic lunch, and that, even if he had come later, she would have figured out some way they could have the picnic.

He was right. With no more foolery they got the picnic basket filled, the gallon thermos into the car, got Donn to the bathroom one last time, and embarked on their trip.

"Where we headed?" asked Evelyn as though she didn't know. Peaceful Point was where they were headed, she was sure. They nearly always went to the same place on these short-trip picnics. There was a spot north on the bay where practically no one else ever seemed to go, where the rocks and sand were uncluttered by either humans or their refuse. You could stay there all day listening to the waves lapping the shores, the gulls crying, and the wind in the trees being the only sounds. They could talk. There was hardly ever any real time to talk at home.

Living in a parsonage was at times like living in a bird cage, Evelyn thought. Part of the time people cooed at you and petted you, and sometimes they even fed you, but there were bars. There were things you'd like to say sometimes, and had to bite your tongue to keep from saying them; there were places you'd like to go sometimes and couldn't because Mrs. Fuddyduddy didn't think it was a suitable place for "Christians." And there were times when you wished you could scream at them all and tell them to go chase themselves. But you didn't. Because you remembered that the people in general were never very kind to Him, either, and if you were going to follow Him, you followed no matter what. And you didn't complain, either. Because most of the time there was that wonderful Presence that overcame the hurts and the tears and the sighs. And sometimes there was real joy, joy that the ones in the world who were not followers knew nothing about. And there were some wonderful fellow travelers along the heaven road.

"How were the Carmichaels?" Evelyn asked now as they drove along the tree-lined bay road toward their favorite spot. She didn't often ask, but she was especially interested in the Carmichaels, Herb knew. And there was nothing particularly confidential about the call, so he told her.

"Did you help them?" she asked then. That was like her, too, Herb thought comfortably. Her concern was genuine. That was what had helped his ministry at Grace Baptist.

"I think so," he answered her slowly. "They were smiling when I left . . . and they were holding hands. That made me feel good."

"Would you like to hold my hand?" she asked, moving closer. But Donn pushed her away, bracing one arm against his father and the other against her chin. "Daddy drive," he said distinctly.

"Later," Herb told her as they both roared. After many head and finger-shakings, and "*no*, daddy's driving," the message had finally gotten through to their young son!

It was a wonderful, happy day. They raced down to the water and sat while Donn picked up pebbles from the beach and made a lopsided sand castle. Then they ate, savoring each bite of the ham-on-rye sandwiches, potato salad and relishes that Evelyn had fixed, draining the lemonade to the last drop, and finally finishing off with Jello for dessert. They didn't have money for steaks, but the air made their appetites keen, and everything tasted wonderful.

After the meal they had time to sit down and talk. They spread their blanket in front of a huge oak tree. They still talked about Herb's dream — a home for "underprivileged" boys and girls. Herb always said the hope of the world tomorrow was the young people of today. They talked about the money it would take for his project, and how it could be organized and set up.

Herb finally slid down on the blanket with his head in her lap, and Donn crept up to her right side and thrust his head under her arm. The first thing she knew her husband was asleep, and her son, also, and there she sat, feeling just slightly resentful. Just like always, Evelyn thought. Here she sat, the two of them asleep in her lap, and she was expected to keep awake, brush the ants off if they strayed too close, and fend off any other dangers that might arise while her warriors slept. She smiled amusedly then. "Well, what else do I want?" she asked herself whimsically. "I've got my man and he's a fine one. And I've got a lovely little girl and a lovely little boy. I'm happy!" she realized suddenly, and a surge of joy shot through her so that she had to restrain herself from whooping outright, and squeezing them both, hard. She lay back, instead, against the trunk of the tree, and day-dreamed.

There was the home visitation program she wanted to see started in the church. Not just calling on their own church members, but reaching out into the community. There were so many homes that didn't have what they had. It wasn't that they lacked material things, she thought, but there was so much bitterness and blindness among people today. She dreamed on, dimly conscious of the twittering of the birds and the hum of a few late honey bees getting nectar from the wild asters blooming along the beach. She thought, *It's fall and I need some new clothes. I need two new dresses. One for "good" and one for shopping, mid-week meetings and the like.* Their budget wasn't very large, but she didn't actually suffer for want of clothes. Sometimes her folks would come over from Adrian in the southern part of the state, and bring her a new skirt and sweater. Or, as they had done one time — a new fall coat.

"Four o'clock! Why, Pam, the poor kid! She'll be home from school and there's no one there!"

She prodded Herb urgently and woke Donn, who was inclined to be cross. "Know what time it is?" she said in an incredulous voice. "I got to daydreaming with you two guys asleep, and it's 4:00."

"Four o'clock?" said Herb, leaping to his feet in a daze. "It can't be. We just got here."

She showed him her watch and then there ensued a wild scramble, packing the picnic dishes into the car, picking up the blanket, gathering Donn's toys together, racing to the car, and then the drive home, much faster than they had come.

"How could we do such a thing?" wailed Evelyn. "What'll we do? Where will she go?"

"Debby will look after her," reassured Herb, hoping he was right. Debby was the next-door neighbor girl, two years older than Pam, who usually saw their little girl to her door. Actually the Gales lived two houses away, as there were two empty lots between them, but they always referred to them as "next-door neighbors." Debby enjoyed playing the part of the older sister to Pam, who was just six, and it eased their minds each day to know that they didn't have to worry about Pam's getting to school and home again all right.

The miles flew by. Herb was driving fast, but the bay road was winding, and the pavement was not too good in spots. Nevertheless, at 5:15 they were home, in record time, and there was no sign of a worried Pam on the doorstep.

They unlocked the door and went in, dropping the picnic basket on the kitchen table, Herb rushed Donn to the bathroom for an emergency trip. "Too much lemonade," he said to Evelyn as they passed her.

Evelyn rushed to the telephone, intending to call Mrs. Gale. The phone started to ring and Evelyn answered it.

In the bathroom, Herb heard her gasp. Heard the break in her voice as she said, "Oh, no! It can't be. It can't. I can't bear it. How awful!"

Herb, realizing that the pain in her voice was real, rushed out of the bathroom door in time to see his wife hold the phone out to him blindly. Tears were sliding down her cheeks, and her face was ashen.

He took the telephone from her. "What is it?" he asked the unknown caller. "Can I help?"

"Oh, Pastor Tabor." The voice at the other end of the line was so broken it was barely recognizable as that of Sandy Jones, the fifth-grade girls' Sunday school teacher. "I've been trying to get you. I can hardly talk. But I must." She choked, then continued. "About two hours ago they found the body of one of my girls. In an empty lot next to the lumber yard in Bayview. She . . . she was murdered. By a sex criminal. It's too awful. I can't bear it."

That's what Evelyn had said, thought Herb. "You mean it was one of our Sunday school pupils?" he asked unbelievingly while mad thoughts chased themselves through his mind. Such things just didn't happen to church people. They just didn't get into situations where things like that happened to them. If you minded your own business and didn't hang around the wrong end of town such things didn't happen. But, Sandy Jones was telling him, something *had* happened.

"Oh, yes," sobbed Sandy. "I told your wife. It was Sally. Sally Ames."

*Sally Ames!* Herb started. A picture flashed into his mind — a picture of a too-short-skirted girl swinging gayly along a city street, her long hair flying behind her in the early morning breeze, her red cardigan sweater billowing behind. He could feel the blood leaving his face, knew he must somehow pull himself together, because ministers didn't faint. Not ever. And they weren't supposed to cry. And they must always have the right answers. Answers? His own mind was so filled with questions he wanted to cry aloud. "Why, God? Why? She was so happy this morning. She was so young. She had her life to live."

Instead, he said merely, "Thank you for calling, Sandy. I'll see what I can do." He hung up the receiver, and just stood beside the telephone, hearing Evelyn crying beside him, and hearing his small son in the bathroom. "Daddy! I'm through, daddy. Come and get me."

"Evelyn." He started toward her and came to a halt,

unable to find the words he wanted to say. "Evelyn," he began again. "It's all right. She is with the Lord."

"Herb," Evelyn said, "you'll have to go . . . the parents. They must have loved her a little, at least. Even if they never showed it. They must. They're human beings."

"Of course," he said. "I'll have to go and offer our services. They have no other pastor."

"If you want, I'll go with you," offered Evelyn. "I can probably get someone to take care of Donn." Having said this she remembered Donn was still in the bathroom. She went to get him.

"I'll go alone for now," Herb told her when she was back. "Remember, we don't know where Pam is, yet."

"That's right," said Evelyn with a little gasp. "We don't. Oh!" Her eyes got wider and terror came into them. "You don't . . ."

"I think she is just fine — somewhere," said Herb without any real conviction.

The telephone rang again. Herb picked it up. It was Dora Gale. "We have Pam here, you know," she said. "It's terrible, isn't it — that little girl. Did you know her?"

"We just heard about it," replied Herb briefly. "She was one of our Sunday school pupils."

"Oh!" said Debby's mother in a stricken voice. "Well, *our* kids are safe, anyway. Nowadays you can never know. Debby will bring Pam over right away."

"Thanks so much, Mrs. Gale," said Herb. "We appreciate it deeply. Evelyn and I went for a picnic later this morning and time escaped us. I went to sleep and Evelyn forgot to wake me in time."

"That's all right, Mr. Tabor. We love your little girl," said Dora Gale.

"Debby will bring Pam over right away," he told Evelyn when he hung up the phone. "I'll go right over to Ameses. I wonder . . . " he began, as new thoughts began to blossom in his mind. "I wonder where she was found, and how long she had been dead . . . the time she was killed."

The unwanted thoughts that came to his mind were

fearful. He pushed them aside. It was best, he thought, to go to the home of the Ameses and try to comfort them if they needed it. He hoped Mr. Ames would be sober.

\* \* \*

The man in the car in front of the paint store on Bay Highway was impatient. He had thought when he came along earlier in the morning he could see the kids walking to school. The girls. Of course the paint store wouldn't open until 9:00. But it made a good place to park, with no one asking any questions. If anyone did ask, he thought, he could pretend that he thought the store opened at 8:30 instead of 9:00. Last week it had been the grocery on Ninth and Terrace, across from the Terrace Elementary School. And before that he had parked occasionally near a swimming pool on the north side of Bayview. Just watching the kids, he was — especially the girls.

He knew that what he was doing was wrong. The voice inside told him that. He had no rest anymore, either in his body or in his mind. Some strange evil had gripped him, and he lived in the midst of it unable or unwilling to do much about it. It was agony on Sundays when the preacher got a little too close to certain subjects of sin. Sometimes he even could feel the sweat break out on him, and he thought it was a wonder his wife hadn't noticed anything wrong. But she was too busy, he thought, to notice much of anything except her own plans for the day. Maybe if she weren't so busy, he would tell himself, and if she paid more attention to him in a wifely way, he would not be experiencing the strange feelings he had had lately.

Even at work he suffered from them. They had started about a year before but had been increasing in intensity and in frequency. There were times lately when he indulged in fantasies when he seemed to be someone else, times when he could imagine himself doing things that were evil. Things that should have caused him to blush with shame, but didn't.

He sat now, looking into his rear-view mirror once in

awhile to see if anyone was slowing down or watching him, and that is how he happened to see Herb Tabor's car stop and let out Sally Ames. He was only five hundred feet away, and he knew Herb's car well. Too well. Just the sight of it now brought back memories of church and preaching . . . and God. It was funny, he thought. God was real to him, just as real as He had ever been. But for some time now he just didn't bother his head about Him. He had come to figure that He didn't care very much one way or another how a man lived. And even if He did . . . well? He was sick and tired of the hypocrisy and cheating among some church members he knew, and while he knew himself to be guilty of some of the very things of which he accused others in his heart, nonetheless he was sick and tired of the whole thing. The whole religious bit.

He waited to see if the pastor was going to be coming his way but sighed with relief when the dark blue car turned down Sandhill Drive.

Now the sight of Sally's miniskirted figure coming down the street toward him made the blood leap in his face. He could feel a pounding in his ears that always presaged the aura of unreality. Today — he had the feeling that some of his fantasies were going to come true. On impulse he started up his car and turned it into the parking lot behind the paint store. He got out quickly, his breath coming faster now, and managed to get to the end of the drive just as Sally was coming along the sidewalk. He knew who she was, of course. Who didn't? He had seen her at church. She certainly had grown up the past year or so, he thought. He pretended that he was just going up to the door of the paint store.

"Hello, Sally," he greeted her rather breathlessly. "How are you? Aren't you late for school?"

"Fine," she told him, answering both questions. "I forgot my geography book this morning and Miss Blackport made me go home after it."

"It's a nice day, isn't it?" the man asked then. "How'd you like to see my puppy?"

"Puppy?" Sally had started to walk by, but now she

25

stopped and looked at him questioningly. "I didn't know you had a puppy, Mr.——."

"Just got it," he interrupted breathlessly, before she had a chance to say his name. "Come on, I'll show you." He took her unresisting arm and she walked with him to the car.

He opened the door and she looked inside. There was no puppy, and now he had to lie again. "I just bought it," he said. "It's right down the block there — just by your school. The woman said I could come after it later today."

"Oh," said Sally in a disappointed voice. "Well, I'll see it sometime, I guess."

"Oh, I'll take you there," he said. "It isn't far. Right by the school. Get in." He forced himself to look away from her.

Obediently she climbed into the car and sat next to the window. She looked at him rather strangely, but no wonder, he thought. The way he was babbling. What was he doing, anyway? How could he ever get this girl to forget he had accosted her, invited her into his car? He didn't own a dog. Hated dogs, in fact. What wild impulse was driving him on? He liked just being near the girl. She was young, young. That was what he liked — the little girls.

He got the car under motion, out on the street again, and turned toward the school. Only, instead of going to the school, he made another turn.

"I'll be awful late," she told him then. "I hope it's a nice puppy."

"It is," he assured her. "You won't be sorry." He made another turn. Now he was headed toward the vacant lot next to the Standard Lumber Company. There was a harder, steadier pounding in his head now, and he felt disembodied, eerie. He was only dimly conscious of the world outside. His world all focused suddenly into one small space — his car, and the young girl and himself. There was no one in the lumber yard, a fact he had been rather certain of beforehand. They didn't open until 10:00. He knew that. In fact, in the past few months he had become well acquainted with the opening times and the closing times of most of the businesses on the north side of Bayview. Since he did not have to be at work until later, he had "cased" most of the schools and most of the businesses in the area.

He turned his car into the driveway of the yard and drove up next to the huge pile of lumber stacked at the rear of the lot. He shut off the motor.

When he turned to face the girl his face was so changed that her tongue seemed to stick in her throat. She felt suddenly paralyzed. He reached for her, and she pushed at him, once, at the same time trying to open the door of the car, but she was too frightened to co-ordinate her muscles. Besides, she had gotten in awkwardly and her skirt was twisted, making it difficult for her to turn again. She tried to scream as she felt his hand on her blouse, but his other hand came up over her mouth tightly, and his face grinned at her wolfishly, while he drew her closer, closer. She fought him for she was a strong little girl, but her strength was no match for his. The other hand left her blouse and closed around her throat.

Sally's frightened brain was registering scattered thoughts. *Why does he want to hurt me? Why did I go with him? It's such a beautiful day. If only Mother had been home when I got there.* It seemed terribly important right now that she see her mother . . . give her some message. Oh, yes. She wanted her mother to know that she loved her. And God . . . that was it! Mr. Tabor. He had said that God looked after her always, and there was no reason ever to be afraid. The pain! She couldn't bear it, but she couldn't scream. She couldn't even breathe. The hand on her throat was cruelly harsh. *God,* she said in her mind, *Jesus, I know You are with me. You always are.* And then, suddenly, He was with her. It was that quick. She sighed once, and the man felt her body go limp in a way that baffled and frightened him. Instantly, he became infuriated.

All this time he had dreamed and dreamed. All this time he had waited. And now this limp rag of a doll, this poorly hatched scion of society, this imp of the devil had outwitted him. She had died, and he wanted her to live. He held her first at arm's length, but any fool could see she was dead, he thought. He struck at her again and again, beating at her face and her body with his fists. It was not enough. There was a flashlight in the car and he used that, striking again and again. Then he opened the car door and pushed her out, into the tall weeds that lined the lumber yard.

He shut the car door and sat up again behind the wheel, trying to compose himself, trying to pull his mind and body together again. His strength seemed spent, passion had died away, and anger, and he felt emptied. Sane! He was sane again. After all, he had a position of some importance. And no little upstart of a girl was going to interfere with his life. He got the car started again, using some automatic reflex action that seemed to be outside himself. He started to drive off, looked down and saw in the seat beside him the bloodied flashlight. Whew! he thought.

He had moved the car a hundred feet when he noticed the flashlight. Stopping the car, he picked the light up gingerly, wiped off the end of it on some paper handkerchiefs he found in the glove compartment, wondering, meanwhile, whose flashlight it was. Of course! An unholy gleam came into his eyes. He turned it over and saw a little black plate fastened to the light with the initials, "H.T." It had been a good light. He started up the car, backed up a few feet and opened his door and threw out the flashlight. It landed somewhere in the weeds near a lumber pile . . . a different pile from where the girl lay. They wouldn't find it, he thought, for a long time, if ever. And even if they did — so what?

He found some matches in the glove compartment and held a lighted match up to the bloody paper in the seat. Holding it away from him while it burned, he threw the remaining scrap of paper away in the air and it fluttered away. He was getting nervous now, for time was passing, and he knew he had to get away. He drove out the driveway, around the block, and saw no one. Then he drove past the school to see if anyone was standing outside, waiting for the girl. No one was. He had thought perhaps they would be looking for her, but no one was in sight. It was only 9:10 now, and he had plenty of time to get to work.

He kept looking down at himself, holding his hands out to see if there were any marks on them — any blood, any signs of a struggle — but he could see none. Perhaps there was a tiny scratch on his left thumb, but it was nothing. It wasn't even bleeding. He straightened his shirt collar and his tie — yes, he had even worn a tie today — and decided he looked fine. As he drove at a measured pace toward work realization came. He was different. He was a *murderer*. From this day on, he would be a hunted man. A strange pride crept over him, a feeling that was new to him. He would fool them. Let them look. They'd never find him.

*       *       *

Elderly Mrs. Vogel probably would never have noticed the car at the paint store if it hadn't been that, just as she was pulling her shade up for the day on the west side of the room, she knocked down a small, plastic-potted ivy from the window.

"Drat it anyway," she said, and bent over to pick it up. Some dirt had gotten on the floor, but mainly, the plant was undamaged. She righted it, fussed around among the leaves a bit and then carefully replaced it in the window. That was when she saw the car, and wondered why a car was parked in front of the paint store at that time. Eight-forty, it was, and too early for the store to open. She was slightly curious so stood a moment watching the man inside the car. She couldn't see him too well because she was nearsighted, and her glasses hadn't been changed in over two years. But she could see that the car had an occupant, and that he was looking in his rear-view mirror as though watching something or someone.

Mrs. Vogel's life lacked excitement. She was a widow and she lived alone and lonely in the square, white, old frame house where her husband had brought her as a bride. A good many years ago it was, and now she was left alone to pass away as best she might lonely hours which were broken only by the sound of children on their way to and from school, and the sight of occasional customers at the paint store. There was something now about the man and the car which riveted her attention. It seemed to her there was something furtive in his manner and she stayed by the edge of the drape, peeking out, certain he was unaware of her scrutiny.

Suddenly, she saw a young girl coming along the sidewalk in front of her house — she could see the red sweater and the long, dark hair. She could see the buoyant walk of the girl and the flounce of the pleated skirt which she wore. Mrs. Vogel sniffed. There did seem to be entirely too much of bare legs showing lately, she thought. It wasn't a good thing at all, she allowed. The girl had stopped and half turned around. While Mrs. Vogel had been watching the girl, she had forgotten to watch the man in the car. He had moved his car, had pulled it into the parking lot behind the store, and now he was walking out to meet the girl. She seemed to know him, smiled and seemed to chat for a moment. Presently, Mrs. Vogel saw the man take the girl's arm, saw the two of them go up the driveway of the paint store, and saw them go up to the car. Strain as she might, she couldn't see around that corner where the window wasn't! She could not see the girl get into the car, but presently she saw the car drive out the driveway and head south, and the girl was in it.

She watched the car until it was out of sight, and saw it turn at Elm Street. Then she could see no more.

She went to take her tea kettle off the stove as it was whistling, and made herself some instant coffee. Then she made toast, all the while thinking about what she had seen. It didn't seem right, some way, and she wished there was someone she could talk to about it. She thought of calling her neighbor, Mrs. Breen, but knew she didn't get up usually until 9:00 or 9:30, because her husband was a night watchman on the 3:00 to 11:00 shift, and they always slept late in the mornings. Well, she could call her daughter and see what she thought about it.

Her blood pressure was always high, and the doctor had told her to keep from getting excited about things. Now she felt slightly faint, and a little dizzy, but she thought it would pass. She went to the telephone and dialed her daughter's number. The line was busy. She held on a moment, hoping the line would clear, but then sighed faintly and hung up. She stepped back, away from the phone, and started to go to the window again. Just as she started toward the window, her toe caught the end of the ottoman that stood by her favorite chair. She tried to catch herself, but felt herself falling. The next moment she had struck the table leg and lay, a slight, huddled figure, strangely crumpled and still.

# 2

THE AMES' HOME was a shack on the north side of Blue-berry Drive, a short, dead-end road in the "no man's land" section between Anchorville and Bayview. It had been built well in its day, but the neglect of man and the elements of nature had combined to make it now an unsightly-looking mess. It was almost literally, a dump. Empty cans, mostly beer cans, were scattered around the doorstep and in the backyard. An old washing machine stood in the backyard; pails and brooms of undetermined use stood near it or were leaning against it. A broken clothesline dragged on the ground and a window screen hung, unrepaired, from a window on the east side of the house.

As Herb arrived at the front door a repulsive odor rushed out to assail his nostrils. It was the unforgettable smell — the odor of the poor. It was an odor he had learned to recognize from his short years as pastor, especially at Anchorville, where, to the west of the town, a small settlement of homes clustered together, sheltering what is loosely termed as the "lower-class citizens." Annoyed but undaunted by the smell Herb stood his ground, remembering that from this home had been salvaged a child of God. And who knew but that He might have more children in that home?

A child came to the door. It was the youngest child of the Ameses, five-year-old Kelly. Her face was tear-streaked and dirty. She recognized Herb and began to sniffle dismally, digging both fists into her reddened eyes. "Mummy. The preacherman's here."

Herb's eyes strained past her into the dim room and at the man and woman who were coming toward him.

"Come in, come in," said the man who was Sally's father. It was the first time Herb had ever seen him sober. Although John Ames still reeked with the fumes of consumed alcohol, Herb could see he was stone sober.

Herb entered the house ill at ease. It was difficult enough to go to any bereaved person when you could talk with him intelligently about a hope for eternity. But to try to speak to parents in such a situation— parents who had openly mocked and belittled the child — what did one say? All the way to their house he had fervently asked the Lord for assistance as he had never in his life felt so inadequate or so helpless.

Just at the moment when he was feeling ready to make a desperate plunge into a proper speech, he saw Sally's mother. She was there, of course, all the time. But all at once, he *saw* her.

Ursula Ames appeared to be in a state of shock and looked as though she hadn't been to bed for several days. Usually not the neatest dresser, she was now disheveled, her clothes hanging crookedly, her hair mussed, her face a wreck. She was not crying now, but she had cried. Mascara stains ran down her face onto her cheeks, cheeks which were the color of paper — dirty, white-gray paper. Her eyes were wide and staring and her hand which held an unlighted cigarette, trembled violently.

If Herb had had any question about whether Ursula Ames had cared for her daughter, he now had his answer. No matter what she had done or said in the past, she was suffering now. The woman before him would, if not given assistance soon, disintegrate into hysteria. And her look at him was pathetic, a mixture of defiance and panic. She expected judgment, he knew. She expected judgment without mercy, as she had meted it out.

A great tide of pity and love rushed over Herb and he could have wept for her. He had come with a hardness in his heart toward them both but it now melted away. For a moment he felt as the Lord must have felt as He viewed the people around Him — great compassion only, and no hate. He took her gently by the sleeve and said, "Let's sit down over here." He steered her toward a davenport which stood against the wall at one side of the room. He sat, and at the same time he became conscious of a fourth adult in the room, a young man of doubtful motive who was sitting forward on the edge of a chair in the other corner, keen-eyed and alert. Herb nodded to him but his main concern was for the woman.

"*Bayview Bugle*," volunteered the young man.

"Pastor Herb Tabor," replied Herb. Then, out of the corner of his mouth, he said, "This is private. Why don't you take a walk?"

Surprisingly, the young man rose obediently and left.

"Reverend Tabor," cried Ursula Ames then. "Will God ever forgive me? Will He *ever* forgive me? Ever since they called this afternoon, I've been out of my mind. It's me who should be dead, instead of her. My poor baby. Oh, God. Oh, God."

Her words had a strange, mechanical utterance as though she had been rehearsing them in her mind and was now saying them aloud for the first time.

"God forgives everyone who asks for forgiveness," said Herb. "And He never goes back on His word."

"I did love her," said Ursula Ames then, brokenly. "But I knew it was wrong I had her, and I didn't want anyone to know that I loved her, because it was a sin, and I should have hated her, but I didn't, really. God took her away to punish me."

"I don't think God took her away to punish you," said Herb slowly. "You see, God chastises only His own chil-

34

dren, and you aren't one of them yet, Mrs. Ames, but you can be, if you want to be.''

"But — my God, when I think how she died,'' whispered the woman. "But they said she died very quickly. You see, she was strangled.'' She broke into ragged sobbing.

Mr. Ames shuffled his feet, He clenched and unclenched his fists futilely. "I ain't much of a man, I guess,'' he said. "But I'd like to get my hands on that . . . that . . . murderer. I ain't much of a man, but I guess I never killed no little girls. The kids was always close to me — part of the time, anyway.'' His eyes slid around to the little one, who was sniveling in the corner. "That-un there. She always comes and climbs on my knee at night when I read the paper. I used to take 'em to the show once in a while. I was good to 'em.''

Mr. Ames went on consoling himself, talking to no one in particular, and in the next room Herb could hear a television set going. There was no one watching it that he could see.

Herb cleared his throat. "Well, I came to convey our deepest sympathy for you both, from myself and my wife, and from the church. My wife sent along the message that, if there is any way at all she can help, she'll be glad to do it. And she means it, too,'' he said firmly.

"My sister is coming later tonight,'' said Mrs. Ames. "She has to come from Indiana. On the train, she is. So there'll be someone here. And they're not going to show her until tomorrow afternoon. They said it would take time to . . . to . . . fix her up.''

"Mrs. Ames,'' said Herb, "I think you should lie down. I think you should have a doctor give you some medication for your nerves. You've sustained a terrible shock, and the next few days will not be easy.''

"No,'' answered Ursula Ames, sitting stiffly before him, "There's nothing ever easy. Not for me, there ain't.'' She sat rigidly for a moment, then her husband spoke up.

"Do like he says, Ursie,'' he urged her. "Lay down. Like he says, it ain't going to be easy.'' He turned to Herb.

"Kinda shaky myself," he said with a sheepish grin.

The newspaper man had returned and was standing loosely in the room near the doorway listening.

Herb got up and Ursula Ames lay back on the davenport and closed her eyes. Herb realized she was near a breaking point. "Who is your doctor?" he asked the father.

"Oh, once in a while we call in Doc Williams," said the man. "He knows us, I guess."

"I think you should call him," said Herb anxiously. He looked over and saw the child Kelly sitting, a rag doll under one arm, her head against the wall, sound asleep. At least she was temporarily out of her misery, he thought.

Ames walked toward the telephone and Herb heard him dialing. There was something he wanted to tell Mrs. Ames and he didn't want it to be painful, but he thought she should know.

"I think you should know, Mrs. Ames," he said, "that your little girl was a real Christian, and that she is in heaven now, with Jesus."

There was no immediate response, so Herb continued, forgetting the man in the doorway. "I picked Sally up, on her way back to school this morning," he said, "and one of the things she said was that she was never afraid of anything, anymore, since she became a Christian last June. She said just this morning to me, 'I'm not afraid anymore. I know Jesus loves me.' "

There was a muffled exclamation from the man near the door, but Herb continued talking. "Mrs. Ames, I wanted you to know that, because it's important. I can tell you on the authority of God's Word that your little girl is safe with her Lord, even now. Now, I'm going to offer a prayer for you, and then I'll leave, and if there is anything you want me to do for you, or anything my wife can do, you let us know." He offered a brief prayer and then left. John Ames accompanied him to the door.

"Thanks for stopping by, parson," he said. "You did help. The doc said he'll come by in a half hour or so."

"Why . . . thank you," said Herb, surprised at Ames'

36

tone. His voice was normal with no alcoholic slur or stutter. On impulse Herb reached out and shook his hand, then turned and went out, walking the short distance to his car. One just never knew, he thought, people kept surprising you continually. He realized, as he drove toward home, that he had not mentioned the funeral to them; perhaps they had already made arrangements with someone else.

*   *   *

The young man standing by the door was suddenly galvanized into action. Without a word to the Ameses, he turned hastily and ran toward his car, jumped in, got it into gear and raced out the driveway. He had been assigned by the *Bugle* to go to the Ames' home in search of some human interest angle of the killing. It hadn't been hard to piece together the sort of home the girl had had. One look had turned his stomach. But work was work. Any murder case was news, and a case of child-molesting was even more so.

Timothy O'Leary sped toward the nearest pay telephone which, he assumed, would be somewhere in the downtown section, what there was of it, in Anchorville. Right. There was a pay telephone near the grocery. He pulled his car to the curb and leaped out, discovering with relief at the last minute that although he didn't have a dime, he did have two nickels.

Excitement had been building in him. He knew he was about to break a real news story. He took the receiver off the hook and put in his nickels, waiting impatiently for the clinging noise that would signify he had the line. Even a split second seemed like forever, right now. He dialed and heard the line open at the other end. *"Bayview Bugle,"* said a pleasant voice.

"Listen, Kate," said Tim O'Leary, speaking rapidly, "I've stumbled onto something that may be really big. It's my big chance. Can you give me some information, quick-like? Atta girl, Kate. I want to know: the Ames girl. She was found in a vacant lot next to a lumber yard, right?" The voice said he was correct. "What time did they find her?" he asked. "Oh, 3:30 this afternoon. Did they say how long she'd been dead?"

His eyes lighted appreciatively as the voice came back to him staccato from the other end.

"Found 3:30 this afternoon in a vacant lot next to the Standard Lumber Company yard. She had been dead for six or seven hours, the coroner said. Died about 9:00 this morning, he figures. She died from strangulation, but was savagely beaten after being strangled. They do not have the weapon that was used to beat her. They think it was done by a sex deviate, although she was not raped."

"Thanks loads, Kate, old friend," said Tim O'Leary. "I'll be in and type up my story in about a half hour. I'll get a bite to eat, and I'll have a story for the morning paper."

"Good going, Tim," said the voice.

He hung up the phone and stepped out of the booth, looking around carefully. Thoughts were popping in his head like firecrackers; his fingers itched to get at his typewriter and type out a feature story that would turn the town upside down. But he was hungry — it was 7:30 — starved, in fact. It was dark outside now, lights gleamed from the Beefburger Hang-out across the street. A hamburger wouldn't consume much of his valuable time, he thought, and it sure would taste good, along with a cup of black coffee. He headed across the street to the Hang-out. Once inside he looked at the menu and decided on a deluxe burger with everything. He needed everything he could get at the fastest possible speed.

While he waited for the waitress to come to him, his thoughts were not on the food. He was forming sentences in his mind. Sentences that would leap out of the page the next morning, shocking citizens out of their complacent lethargy. Tim was a tough young man, and he didn't shock easily, but he liked to shock others. This time he would have a real shocker, he thought.

The waitress came and took his order and he waited for its preparation impatiently, muttering softly to himself now and then and gazing into the distance while his mind pulled out and mulled over little details he had heard. Yes, sir, he thought, the people could be prepared for a real tear-jerker tomorrow. Around him people were talking, talking. He could hear bits of conversations.

"Awful, isn't it?"

"Nobody's safe anymore."

"Her father . . . drunk. Her mother. . . ."

O'Leary realized he had chosen a place that was a hotspot of civic indignation. Just a short distance from the girl's home, the center of Anchorville was in a state of fear, shock and suppressed fury.

"Cops," said one woman. "They don't do much nowadays. Just there for looks. Never know what is going to happen anymore."

On impulse, O'Leary got up out of his booth and walked over to a table around which were seated four women. "I'm new around here," he said. "What's all the excitement about?"

"A murder," answered four voices as one. He had difficulty sorting out the voices, difficulty making out sentences. They were all pouring at him rapidly, jerkily. "Poor kid . . . father drinks all the time . . . mother's a no-good bum . . . waitress at the tavern . . . kid's illegitimate . . . mother hates her, everybody knows it . . . poor kid, never had a chance . . . Sally was big for her age, probably would have been just like her mother — no good."

Tim sat down on one corner of the booth next to the table. "That's interesting," he said. And listened while they poured more news and gossip into his ready and waiting ears.

"You say she was adopted?" he asked, a trifle bewildered by all the versions of history thrown at him.

"No! Not adopted," said a large, red-faced woman in a too-tight dress. "She's her mother's girl, but not her father's."

"I see," said Tim, enlightened now as the truth began to dawn upon him. "You say she was not well treated?"

"Her mother hated her," said the red-faced woman. "I used to say to her, 'Why don't you adopt her out, seeing's how you don't like her?' But she never would hear of it."

Tim O'Leary straightened his shoulders and shook his head. "Poor little kid," he said truthfully. "Poor little kid."

"You can say that again," said the women as with one voice.

Tim went back to his own booth thinking harder than ever. What he had hold of here was a real hot one . . . not only was the girl murdered in a distasteful way, but her whole life had been one of abject misery, he thought. He wolfed down the hamburger which arrived and swallowed his coffee greedily, knowing he needed the food, but impatient to get the story. He knew exactly what he was going to write.

Back at the *Bugle* offices he sat down at his typewriter without even pulling off his light jacket. Without paying attention to anyone he typed forcefully, beating out the words that were erupting inside him. At 9:30 P.M. he handed the sheets across the desk to his boss, Bert Stankiewicz.

Bert began to read the sheets, stiffened suddenly, looking at Tim with eyes that bored through him. "What you wrote — is it true?"

Tim nodded in the affirmative. The other man looked at him steadily. "You aren't withholding evidence?"

Tim shrugged. "They'll find out in due course anyway. It is only a matter of time."

"Okay. This is good writing. You're getting better. Man!" He tossed the sheets back to Tim. "Okay, finish it off. We'll hit the town with it in the morning."

\* \* \*

When Herb got home again it was 7:30 and Evelyn had fed the children, but there were two plates at the table, and she had fixed a hot supper, a 'quickie" casserole, as she called it, with macaroni, cheese, tuna and green peas. It was by no means Herb's favorite dish but he counted himself indeed fortunate to have anything hot at this time of night, especially after a shock such as Evelyn had had, and he was grateful even for the casserole.

"Thanks for waiting for me, honey," he said. "It's been such a strange day . . . on top of the mountain this afternoon. Now the valley."

"I know," she said, gazing at him with compassion. "I put the kids to bed early. I figured you'd want to talk about it."

He asked a blessing on the food then waited while she dished out onto his plate from the casserole. "It's too hot to pass," she said.

He wondered why he could not say what he had to say. The thought had been hanging ominously over him for two hours now and it was depressing. He found he could not relish his food, and his stomach was tense. It should have been so simple, but it was not.

"What's the matter, Herb?" asked Evelyn quietly. She laid down her fork and surveyed him with anxious eyes. "You aren't ill, are you?"

"I guess I'm afraid," he confessed, looking her straight in the eyes.

"Afraid?" she said in amazement. "Afraid of what?"

"Evelyn," he said tensely. "I was probably the last person on earth, with the exception of the murderer himself, to see Sally Ames alive."

"What?" Evelyn's tone was thin, high. "I don't understand."

Herb spoke in a carefully controlled voice. "Honey, as I was driving in to Bayview this morning to see the Carmichaels, I saw Sally Ames walking along the road. I very seldom pick someone up, but she seemed in a hurry, and I stopped and gave her a ride."

"Oh!" The one word was expressive.

"She had forgotten her geography book and the teacher had sent her home after it, she said. She had gotten the book and was on her way back to school again when I picked her up. She looked great — not frightened, or anything, as though anyone had been bothering her. She said, in fact — and it's kind of strange, now that I think of it — that she wasn't afraid to go home anymore now, because she knew Jesus was looking after her."

"Oh." Another tone now, hushed, and with a quaver in it.

"I told her that was wonderful, and left her off at the corner of the highway and Sandhill Drive in Bayview. This is what bothers me. There is such a short gap there. I left her off within a block and a half of the school. She must have been killed within minutes of the time I left her off."

"Herb. Darling," said Evelyn. Her face had turned pale.

"What really worries me," said Herb slowly, unburdening himself, and feeling some of the pressure leaving him, "is that there was a reporter there tonight from the *Bayview Bugle*. He was standing in the doorway at the Ameses when I told Mrs. Ames that I had seen Sally this morning, and he made a kind of exclamation when I said that. I have a feeling he is going to put all this in the paper."

Evelyn stared at him, stricken. She said nothing. What was there to say after all? He was a man in a very unenviable position, and that was all there was to it.

Herb picked up his fork again and forced himself to eat. At least it was off his chest now and Evelyn knew the worst. He was sure that they had only begun to hear about the murder of Sally Ames. He managed to eat half the food on his plate before the telephone rang. Still chewing, he arose from the table to answer it.

"Pastor Tabor?" The voice was a woman's, hoarse and unfamiliar to him. "I'm Mrs. Ames' sister, Mrs. Schwartz, from Indiana. They forgot to ask you tonight, if you would have the funeral."

"Oh, yes, of course!" said Herb. "I — that is actually why I went to see the Ameses tonight, but your sister was really in no condition to discuss the matter, so I told her husband to call a doctor for her, and as I started home again, I realized I hadn't learned what I went there to find out."

"Well, they want you to have the service, if you will. It is to be Thursday afternoon at 1:30. And . . . maybe you'll think this is a little strange, Mr. Tabor, but they would like to have Sally buried from the church. You know what I mean?"

"Yes, of course," answered Herb. "You mean to have the funeral itself in the church."

42

"That's right."

"Certainly," said Herb. "Sally was a member of our church, and it is only fitting and proper that the service would be there. Are there any instructions?"

"No, only Ursula said that Sally loved one of the hymns she sung there, and they would like to have it sung at her funeral."

"What was that, Mrs. Schwartz?" asked Herb mechanically.

"Jesus Loves Me."

At the words, tears started to Herb's eyes. He swallowed hard and managed to say, somewhat gruffly, "That would be all right."

"Is that all right?" his caller asked somewhat haltingly. "You sound so strange. Have I offended you in some way, Mr. Tabor?"

"No — not at all," assured Herb. "It's very . . . touching, that's all. I'll see to it that arrangements are made, Mrs. Schwartz, for the funeral in the church, and I'll have someone sing that song for the Ameses."

"Thank you so much, pastor. We'll appreciate it. Good-by."

"Good-by," echoed Herb, and he replaced the receiver gently. He stood for a moment, staring at the floor. "I don't know," he said, half to himself. "Do they realize . . . "

"What is it, Herb?" asked Evelyn anxiously. She came over and wound her arms around him tightly.

"Evelyn . . . can you imagine this . . . they not only want me to take the funeral, but you know what song they want sung? At the funeral of a little girl who was strangled by a sex deviate?" The drama of it hit him again as he stared at her.

"Tell me, Herb."

"Jesus Loves Me."

"Oh!" Eyes wide, Evelyn stared back at him, dropped her arms and stood back. "They can't."

"It's what they want," said Herb. "Can you imagine?"

"I think it's wonderful," said Evelyn. "But there'll be a lot of people. . . ."

"Who won't approve," finished Herb for her.

"Evelyn," Herb reached out for her. "Please come and sit by me on the davenport, and let's talk. I don't care about eating. Maybe I can eat a bite later. I need to talk. I need to think things out." They sank onto the davenport and Herb sat forward, leaning his arms on his knees and his head on his hands.

"Never before," he said, "never before have I questioned God. There was never any reason to. But this — this has really hit me, hard. Does God *really* love us, Evelyn? Does He really love a little girl like Sally Ames, when He allows things like this to happen? *Does* He?"

"He does," said Evelyn staunchly. "Herb . . . it's awful, of course . . . sickening. But — it really isn't any worse than some of the people who die in auto accidents, is it? They're just as dead. And some of them don't die gently, either. We don't question that."

"No," said Herb. "But this is different. It's so . . . indecent . . . so shocking."

"But — not really, Herb. Maybe she died quickly. She must have, if the coroner is correct and she died at 9:00 or 9:15. She couldn't have suffered much at all, actually."

"I suppose so," said Herb. "Where did you get all that information about the time of death?"

"Radio broadcasts tonight while you were gone," she said. "That's about all that's on WLBV."

"I can imagine," he said. He could still feel the tension in his middle section, could still feel the curious ache near his heart. He could not say why he had this. He hadn't been that close to Sally. But it must be because he still carried fresh in his mind a picture of her as she strode down the sidewalk that morning, her dark, long hair swinging and her red sweater flowing behind her. So buoyant, so alive . . . so young. And God? He had been watching, had seen some vile wretch of humanity reach out and brutally strangle and assault her, and had done nothing. Why? Why?

"I can't bear it," he said. "Supposing it had been Pam?"

"Herb," said Evelyn then, shakily, "don't say such things. But I've . . . I've been thinking that ever since Sandy called us. God couldn't be so cruel as to. . . ." She stopped, gasped. "Herb." She turned and buried her face in his arm.

"See what I mean?" Herb reached out his arm and drew her into it. "God couldn't be so cruel, you say, as to let our Pam die in such a fashion, but it is all right for Him to let Sally Ames die in such a fashion."

"No! No! Herb, I didn't mean it that way," said Evelyn, breaking down finally. "Herb, we aren't doing the right thing, questioning like this. What God does is right. He makes no mistakes. He is just and holy."

"He is just and holy," repeated Herb after her obediently. "You know, Evelyn, you sound just as I might, if I were comforting someone. You should have been a preacher's wife."

"I've thought about it," said Evelyn, trying hard to smile at him through her tears. "But the hours are too long and the pay is too small, and I don't think I could manage on so little."

"The wages you reap are not in money," said Herb tenderly, drawing her closer to him. "You reap only love."

"Mommy! Mommy!" the call came piercing from Pam's room. "Mommy! I want you to help me. I'm scared."

Evelyn sighed and got up reluctantly. She dried her eyes on a corner of her apron as she went toward her daughter's room.

"What is it, chick?" she asked, bending over the small bed.

"Mommy, I'm scared. Nobody's going to get me, are they?"

"Of course not, darling," murmured Evelyn. She was alarmed at the sight of Pam who was sitting up in bed, eyes wide and frightened. "Whatever makes you ask that?" she finished lamely.

"Debbie's mother said we should hurry home tonight,

45

so no one would bother us," said Pam, reaching out her arms to be held.

"No one's going to bother you," said Evelyn as she cuddled the child close. "You go to sleep, darling, because God is watching over you."

"Wasn't He watching over Sally Ames?" asked Pam. Her eyes strained into Evelyn's, searching for an answer.

"Yes, of course," answered Evelyn mechanically. "He watches over us all."

"But she . . . she's dead, isn't she?"

"Yes, but He was still watching over her," replied Evelyn. She fought for words to reassure her little girl. "He just decided that it was time He took Sally home to heaven where she could have all the lovely things she never had down here."

"Oh," said Pam softly. "Will He give her a bicycle, up there, do you think, Mommy?"

"Well," Evelyn considered the problem, seeing that she had drawn Pam's attention away from the terrible present to a glorious future. "I don't really think she'll need a bicycle up there, honey. But whatever is right for her, God will give her."

"God is good," said Pam. Her eyes began to close, slowly. As Evelyn watched, Pam drifted into sleep, deep and peaceful. Thankfully, Evelyn turned away. She realized that her heart was light. In some wonderful way God had come into the room, and was there. Behind her she saw her husband.

"Thanks for the sermon," he whispered. Arms tightly about each other, they turned toward their own room.

"God is here," Evelyn finished. "I'm well, darling. Let's call it a day."

*That's what my pay is,* she thought somewhat wistfully. *I reap only love.*

46

# 3

THE *Bayview Bugle* was now in the hands of the citizens of that city and other cities in the surrounding territory, including the smaller towns of Anchorville, Wade and Torrance.

Headlines screamed the news in bold face: GIRL'S BODY FOUND IN VACANT LOT: SEX DEVIATE SOUGHT IN LOCAL AREA. Underneath the bold type was a picture — last year's school picture — of Sally Ames. She was a pretty girl and, although that should have made no difference to anyone at all, it most certainly did. "And such a *pretty* girl," they would invariably say, holding the paper close to see her better. And, "How awful! And her mother was *working*, of course." This last in spite of the fact that practically everyone's mother did work nowadays, and hardly anyone got murdered because of it. With sadistic intensity people picked up the paper and read and read. It was all there: Sally's father drank and was not much good at holding jobs. Her mother worked all night as a barmaid at Dunbar's, and had not come home that morning yet at 8:15 when the girl had returned home for the book.

The family, the article said, had not treated Sally well at

all, due to the fact that she was a "love child," and not really her father's daughter, although no one had ever seen the father mistreating her. It had rather been the mother who had punished the girl severely, sometimes ridiculing her before friends. And when readers reached the last paragraph, they would begin to click the roofs of their mouths with their tongues and say, "Imagine that. That really doesn't surprise me. Would you believe it," and various other indefinite and non-shocked remarks. "I sure hope they get him," would be the final comment, almost without exception.

The *Bayview Bugle* that same day carried another news item that was smaller and that went practically unnoticed amid the excitement over the murder of Sally Ames. The notice read:

> This morning, Mrs. Esther Vogel, a widow residing on Bay Highway, suffered injuries from an apparent fall. Police investigated after her daughter was unable to get an answer to a telephone call about noon. Mrs. Vogel was taken by police ambulance to Bayview General Hospital, and is in serious condition with apparently severe head injuries. Mrs. Vogel is seventy-six years old and lives alone. The house had not been broken into, and it was thought she fell and struck her head on the table near which she was found. No foul play is suspected, although police are still investigating.

*     *     *

On Tuesday morning Herb made arrangements for the funeral which would be held on Thursday. He enlisted the aid of the church organist, Winifred Carson, for the organ music, and then asked Sandy Jones if she would sing the requested "Jesus Loves Me."

"Think you can do it?" he questioned Sandy, knowing it would be a terrific strain on her already strained emotions.

"If I could sing somewhere besides up front, where I can't see the casket, I'll be able to," said Sandy, a break in her voice. "But otherwise. . . ." Her voice trailed off.

"I think something can be arranged," said Herb. They decided that Sandy would sit off to one side near the organ and behind a screen. The song would then come through clearly, but she would be unseen.

"It's going to be a real weepy one," said Herb. "If you can sing without crying, maybe I can preach a dry sermon."

"I'll try," quavered Sandy. She still looked pale, and her eyes showed dark shadows. She had taken it hard, Herb knew. She was one of those dedicated Sunday school teachers who really loved her pupils.

The matter was settled. Herb wondered how many flowers there would be a funeral like that. He had their Flower Fund chairman order an unusually large bouquet of whatever flowers she wished. At least, he thought, the church would be represented. He found, on arriving at the funeral home, he needn't have been concerned. When he entered that afternoon Sally's casket was surrounded by baskets, potted plants, chrysanthemums, gladioluses, roses. The casket was covered with a spray of pink roses. The card said, "Beloved daughter and sister."

Herb felt choked. There was a lump in his throat so large he felt he could reach in and pull it out. It became suddenly necessary for him to reach into his pocket and take out the clean white linen handkerchief Evelyn had provided for him just before he left the house. He forced himself to go up and look at the child.

Her face was peaceful, but it didn't look much like Sally Ames! Not as she had looked yesterday morning — was it only yesterday — swinging down the sidewalk with youthful buoyancy. Her face had been slightly flushed then, with the wind-pinked cheeks of the healthy child, and her eyes had sparkled. Now they were sightless, lids properly down, as though she slept. Indeed, Herb reminded himself sternly, she was not dead, she was sleeping. The thought came to him suddenly that as yet he had made no effort toward the preparation of a funeral message. It was a horrifying thought, worse than any he had had thus far.

At thirty-one Herb had preached a few services for the dead. Mostly they had been for older persons who had died rather peacefully after a full life. He had once preached a service for a man without a church, and a service for one man who had been killed in an automobile accident. But how did a man stand up and preach the funeral service of a little girl who had been murdered by a sex deviate? Once again, Herb felt overcome by a strange depression. He shook it off, closing his eyes momentarily for a brief prayer.

The parents were there, dressed neatly, and looking surprisingly like other people. Herb, of course, had never seen either of them "dressed up," and was pleasantly surprised that they made as good an appearance as they did. He shook hands with them both, murmuring a few words of appropriate comfort. "Anything you want us to do," he repeated, "we'll be glad to do."

"Thank you," Ursula Ames said quietly. Herb guessed that the doctor had made his call and, through the ministry of a modern-day miracle, had brought a peace of sorts through the remedy of tranquilizing drugs. Her eyes were reddened, and her cheeks slightly swollen, but otherwise she looked better than Herb had ever seen her. She was neat. Her hair had been done at a beauty shop and the dress she had on was adequate for the occasion.

The sister, Mrs. Schwartz, was with her, and was another surprise, for she looked like quite a sharp person, and was stylishly dressed in good clothes. "You are the lady who called me last night?" Herb asked, appraising her quickly.

"Yes, Pastor Tabor. I'm Ursula's sister, Angela Schwartz."

Herb conveyed to them simply the arrangements he had made for the service on Thursday and assured them that everything would be taken care of. "You have a lot of beautiful flowers," he remarked as he prepared to leave.

"Yes — isn't it wonderful?" Angela Schwartz said. "There are flowers here from persons they never even heard of . . . don't know at all, but they just sent them out of kindness."

Herb nodded silently, thinking to himself that these people needed all the kindness they could get.

* * *

At home again, he confronted Evelyn in the living room. "You know what?" he asked, sitting down tiredly in the chair. "Until I walked in the door of that funeral home and looked around, I had completely forgotten that I had a funeral message to prepare. And it isn't going to be an easy one to give."

"No, it isn't," agreed Evelyn sympathetically. "You know, Herb, there is one verse I wish you could use. It just keeps coming back to me, over and over again. It's something like 'Precious in the sight of God is the death of His saints.' At least, that's the gist of it. It makes death sound so — so — comfortable, some way, and especially for a child. And Sally was one of His saints, Herb. She really believed."

"I know she did," he answered thankfully. "That is what keeps me from being really depressed. I guess that must be why the Bible says, 'in everything give thanks.' Because you can usually think of something worse that might have happened. And that would have been that this had happened two years ago, or even one year ago, before she made a commitment to Christ."

Evelyn came over and sat on the edge of the chair near him. "Honey, I want to do something for the Ameses," she said. "But what? Do you think we could have them over for dinner? After the funeral, I mean. When they need something to take their minds off themselves."

Herb looked up at her, loving her with all his being. "You're the greatest," he said huskily. "I love you. Did you know that?"

She leaned over and kissed his cheek. It was almost a friendly kiss, with no passion or intent of passion. Herb thought suddenly that, in a very real sense, that was exactly what he and Evelyn were — friends. It was a wonderful thought. He knew of a great many persons not too far removed from him, who had based their marriages largely on passion. Now they weren't happy, because of widely varying interests and personalities. But the love between Evelyn and him was so deep that now, after eight years of marriage, they were still friends. He still enjoyed talking with her, just as he had before their marriage. Further, they weren't afraid to sit down together in the same room to read, or to be in separate rooms, because there was no gnawing feeling that the other was being cheated, or ignored or punished.

All these thoughts flashed through his mind as he looked at her, smiling. "I think they'd like that," he said, after a moment. "I'll ask them tomorrow."

"No, I'll ask them," she corrected. "Otherwise they may think that I didn't want them and you were the one. . . ." She looked kitchenward and slid gracefully from the side of the chair. "Bye now," she said. "I have to go to the kitchen and think what to have for supper."

"Right on all counts," said Herb. He sank in the chair, eyes closed, thinking. After a time he rose, got his Bible and went to his study. In the study he got down on his knees as was his custom, and prayed. He was grateful that, after all the turmoil of the night before, peace had come, and he was happy that he now found no difficulty in speaking to the Lord about his need.

A half hour later he was well on his way toward preparing the funeral message. He thought that very simply he would tell of Sally's background, how she had come to church through a Vacation Bible School project, and how she had made a confession of faith in Christ, and had been received into membership in the church. And the climax, he thought, would be when he told them what Sally had told him only yesterday. Closing his eyes, he could see her sitting there beside him in the car, could still hear her words plainly: "You know, Mr. Tabor, yesterday you said that God always looks after us, and cares for us. I know He does. I know Jesus loves me, because now I'm not afraid anymore when I go home. I used to be afraid every night, but not now. Not since last June."

Herb came down from his study at 5:30 P.M. and looked around for the paper. He realized he hadn't seen the paper since the morning of the day before. The *Bayview Bugle,* which came out early morning, today would carry the story of the murder. Herb could hear Evelyn working in the kitchen, and Donn was with her. He could hear the childish voice.

"Mama. Whus zat?"

"That's a pork chop. Pork chop."

"Por-rk chup."

"That's right, doll, 'pork chop.' "

"Donn's hungry."

"Daddy's hungry too, doll. You be a good boy and keep out of the way."

Rested by the normal sounds of his household, Herb found the paper and relaxed back into his chair with it, starting, as was his own peculiar custom, at the back of the paper, with the obituaries. There it was, the first one:

> AMES, Sally Irene. Aged ten years. Beloved daughter of Mr. and Mrs. John Ames, Blueberry Drive, N.W. Anchorville, who passed away very unexpectedly Monday morning. Funeral services at 1:30 P.M. Thursday at the Grace Baptist Church, Anchorville, the Rev. Herbert Tabor officiating. Burial in Woodbine Cemetery, Anchorville. Those wishing to call at the funeral home may do so between 2:00 and 4:00 P.M. and between 7:00 and 9:00 P.M. Tuesday and Wednesday. Body is at the Hoekstra Funeral Home.

So that was it. Death was so very final, Herb thought, especially if you had no Christian hope. But for the Christian . . . . He thought that, even now, Sally Ames was in the presence of her Lord. He turned the pages of the paper, scanning the various news items, and finally came to the front section. There it was! Headlines on the front page: GIRL'S BODY FOUND IN VACANT LOT: SEX DEVIATE SOUGHT IN LOCAL AREA. And there was the picture. Herb realized that he had tensed up again unconsciously, and that he had held himself back from turning immediately to the front page.

After all, he reasoned, that would have been the normal thing to do, wouldn't it? He began reading and read the article rapidly. The sharp young reporter had done a good job writing a difficult piece, Herb decided. Then he hit the last paragraph. Or, more to the point, the last paragraph hit him. He realized also that actually he had been expecting this, had unconsciously braced himself for it.

> The only clue to the killing so far is that the last person to see the girl alive was her pastor, the Rev. Herbert Tabor, who made the statement that he had picked her up as she was on her way back to school. Tabor said he let the girl off at the corner of Sandhill Drive and Bay Highway. No one is known to have seen the child after that.

Herb could feel the tightness starting again in his middle. He realized that his teeth were clenched. He didn't know why he should be so apprehensive. No one had called, or made any mention of the matter at all. He lay back in the chair and tried to think calmly. He couldn't recall having seen any cars in the vicinity at all when he stopped to let Sally out. If she had been picked up so soon afterward, the car of the murderer must have been seen in the area already, he thought. He tried to picture the scene in his mind again: the corner where he had let Sally out of the car, the sidewalk, the red shadow of the school a block and a half down the street. But he failed completely to resurrect any buried gleam of evidence that would help. He realized he had had his mind on other things, and actually had paid scant attention to Sally. He had been thinking of the Carmichaels, wondering what they had to see him about. And he had been thinking about the picnic that he and Evelyn and Donn intended to go on later in the morning. Now she had become dominant above everything else. He heard a car door slam out on the street and a moment later the doorbell rang.

"I'll get it," he called to Evelyn, and laying the paper down, he hurried to the door.

On the doorstep were two policemen! "Rev. Herbert Tabor?" asked the older one who, Herb judged, looked to be fortyish. He nodded affirmatively.

"That is correct. Can I help you?"

"Sorry to bother you at supper time," said the officer. "In fact, I'm sorry we have to bother you at all . . . but the fact is . . . can we come in?"

"Of course," replied Herb as heartily as he could. "You've come about Sally Ames, I suppose."

"Right," said the man. "Name's Larson. Bayview Homicide. This is Lieutenant Bailey." He looked behind him then sank into the nearest chair. Lieutenant Bailey took the one opposite. Herb reseated himself in the chair he had just vacated, and waited.

"See the paper today?" asked Larson.

Herb nodded. "Just did. I saw my name mentioned, and right on the front page, too." He forced a grin. "It didn't sound very good, the way it was stated."

"Mr. Tabor," said the officer, "believe me, I hate to say this. You look like a nice young man. But you are our only suspect. What I mean is," he restated his words in a more precise manner. "What I mean is, we have no other suspect at all. The killer left a clean trail behind him. We'd like you to answer a few questions, if you will."

"Certainly," answered Herb. He breathed a little more freely. There was nothing at all ominous or menacing in the manner of either of the officers. "Anything I can say or do to help, I will do."

Evelyn came in from the kitchen, and saw the men. Her mouth flew open and her eyes widened.

The two men stood, and Herb introduced her. "Just a routine check," said the officer. With a nod of his head he politely dismissed her, and she retreated into the kitchen.

"The reporter who wrote the story for the *Bayview Bugle* called our office this morning, and reported to us that last evening he heard you tell the parents that you had picked up Sally Ames on her way back to school. Mind telling us about it?" His tone was friendly enough, but his eyes were hard on Herb's, piercing.

"Well," said Herb slowly, "I left home about 8:30 on Monday to drive to Bayview to see one of our church couples

55

who had requested a counseling session.'' Here he was interrupted by the Lieutenant.

"Names?"

"Jim and Donna Carmichael."

"Okay. Go ahead."

"Well," continued Herb slowly, "I was in somewhat of a hurry, because it was really a nice day, and you know that a minister doesn't get off on picnics very often! My wife and I had planned to go to Bay Point, about forty miles away for a picnic later in the morning. Also, I was in a hurry, because Donna Carmichael had told me her husband had an appointment at 10:15 in the morning, so I wanted to allow plenty of time for whatever they had, and still leave their place early enough to let him keep his appointment."

"What time did you leave their place?" asked the older man.

"Why . . . I think it was somewhere around 9:45," said Herb thoughtfully. "I recall looking once at the clock and thinking that we had to be done, so Jim could keep his appointment."

"The girl was killed around 9:00," said the Lieutenant softly.

"So the paper stated," said Herb.

"Can these people verify your time there?" asked the man who had said he was Larson.

"Well . . . they can certainly tell you that I was there in the early morning," replied Herb. "I can't say positively that they will remember the exact time. I hope they can," he added somewhat drily.

"Yes. Well — get on with your story," said Larson.

"I was just getting up a good speed on Bay Highway," went on Herb, "when I saw Sally Ames walking along with a book in her hand. I don't make a practice of picking up people, but it seemed to me that she was hurrying, and that she probably was late, so . . . I pulled over and asked her if she wanted a ride."

"Just a minute," interrupted the younger man again. "You stopped the car. What did you say to her?"

Herb wrinkled his forehead in an effort to remember. "I think I said, 'Want a lift?' "

"What did she say?"

Herb thought some more. "She said, 'Oh, sure.' Then, after she got into the car she said, 'Boy, am I glad you came along. I got to school early, and would you believe — Miss Blackport sent me home to get my geography book. I'm tired.' "

"I see," said Larson. He was writing rapidly in a red-covered book. "Did she look tired?"

"No," said Herb, smiling. "It takes quite a lot of exercise before a ten-year-old shows fatigue."

"Right," agreed the officer. "Did she seem to be upset, as though she had been bothered at all by anyone on the way?"

"Not at all," answered Herb positively. "I asked her if she had indeed walked all the way to school, then all the way home, and part of the way back, and she said yes. She said she didn't mind, because it was a nice morning." He realized, suddenly, that he was instinctively holding something back, something he didn't want brought out in the papers — at a trial. The girl had said, "And mother wasn't home, so I didn't mind." But they didn't need to know that she had said that. There was enough muck already raked up for people to read. He realized that Larson was looking at him keenly. "That was it," he said shortly.

"The reporter said that you told the parents that she made the statement that she wasn't afraid anymore, because God always looks after us, like you said."

"That's right," answered Herb.

"You find that incompatible with what happened afterward?" asked the officer.

"Not really," said Herb. "I know that to us it seems like an awful way for a little girl to die. But actually, many children die after suffering for months with cancer and other painful diseases. It is never easy to see a child suffer, but suffering is a part of this world."

"I see," said the man. He coughed sharply and turned again to his notebook.

"I see," he said again. "Now then. You say you picked her up. What then?"

"Well," said Herb, wishing he could think of a more intelligent way to begin his sentences, "I saw that it would take me out of my way a few blocks if I took her all the way to the school, so I let her out on the corner of Sandhill Drive and Bay Highway."

"Did you see any other car in the area at all?" asked Larson.

"No," said Herb ruefully. "I was sitting here just before you came, trying to recall if I had seen any other car in the vicinity. I just don't remember."

"She must have been picked up soon after you let her out," remarked Larson.

"Yes," said Herb.

"Remember seeing any cars behind you at all? Did anyone pass you just as you let her out? Was anyone in front of you?"

Herb tried to think, tried to visualize the scene, and once again he failed. "I just don't recall any," he said.

"Then — there are no witnesses to the fact that you let Sally Ames out of your car at the corner of Sandhill Drive and Bay Highway."

"That's right," replied Herb, fighting off a sudden dryness in his mouth, and a sudden constriction in his throat. "I'm afraid — that's right."

"Did the girl seem frightened at all, or uneasy?" asked Lieutenant Bailey.

"Not at all," answered Herb, wondering why the man asked the same question the second time. "She was as happy as could be."

"Then why," said the man, looking at Herb piercingly again, "why did she make that statement about not being afraid anymore?"

"Officer," said Herb, "you don't know the kind of home Sally Ames came from. Her father drinks. Her mother was — was not always kind to her."

"I see. Did the mother mistreat her?"

"Yes," answered Herb briefly.

"What were her last words to you?"

" 'See you next Sunday!' " said Herb. Tears sprang to his eyes as he recalled the happy words.

"Well," remarked Larson, getting heavily to his feet. "Thank you for your time, Mr. Tabor. We're doing everything we can to run this down, but right now it looks as though we are up against a stone wall."

Herb rose also and walked to the door with them. "If I remember anything at all that will help, I'll let you know," he told them. "Good night."

"Good night," they echoed, disappearing rapidly down the walk into the September twilight. He heard the car door slam, and the sound of the police car as it moved away. He walked back to his chair.

"Is it all right?" asked Evelyn anxiously as soon as he sat down.

"I'm still here," he pointed out to her, smiling. "And I'm hungry." Suddenly, he realized it was true. The men were gone and he was free. He got up, walked out to the kitchen, swung Donn up to his high chair and swung Pam in a circle before allowing her to seat herself at the table. She rewarded him with a brilliant smile.

"Dear Lord, we thank You for this wonderful food," prayed Herb, "and for being with us this day. Bless it now as we eat, and help us live lives pleasing to Thee. Amen."

Halfway through the meal, the telephone rang. Herb groaned but got up to answer it.

"Pastor Tabor?" he did not immediately recognize the voice. "Pastor, I read that in the paper today — about you and Sally Ames. I think it's terrible, what they said. It was — it sounded as if you — " The voice went on and on, and Herb wearily held the phone away from his ear. He recognized the voice now as belonging to his long-winded but kind-hearted member, Mrs. Thompson. "Anyhow," that good soul advised him as he prepared to hang up, "I don't believe a word of it, and I wanted you to know it."

"Thank you, Mrs. Thompson," answered Herb softly. He heard the click of the receiver on the other end of the line, and hung up gratefully. Fifteen minutes had passed. His dinner was cold.

"That was the first one," he said to Evelyn. "There will be more."

Ten minutes later, there was. "Pastor Tabor?"

"Yes," said Herb numbly, waiting for the next onslaught of words.

"Pastor Tabor, I want you to know that my wife and I are behind you. We know you — we know the Ameses. We believe in you." The man's voice, Herb recognized, belonged to one of his deacons, Ernest Rhodes. "I appreciate that," said Herb, and hung up again, as there seemed to be no further conversation forthcoming from either of them. It was a strange, quiet moment.

"We could take the phone off the hook," suggested Evelyn seriously, but with an impish smile.

"No — we can't," answered Herb swiftly. "Because we just might get an emergency call."

The instrument rang again. "Pastor Tabor?"

"Yes," said Herb, automatically bracing himself.

"We had to take my Tommy to the hospital this afternoon for an emergency appendectomy. He's not very good, pastor. Would you?"

"Of course!" answered Herb almost happily, in spite of the seriousness of the news. He was so profoundly grateful that this person needed him as a pastor — as a person — that she had called. He knew that Tommy Evans was not very strong, and that an emergency appendectomy just might finish him. He had diabetes, and was never strong, at best. "What hospital is he in?"

"Bayview General," said Mrs. Evans. "Thank you so much."

Herb put down the phone. "I'll have to go to the hospital," he said to Evelyn. "That was for real. See what I mean?" He hastily finished his pie, and looking at his watch saw it was 7:15. He had just time to make the run into

Bayview to see the boy. By the time Herb had visited the hospital and returned home again, it was 9:30, and he decided to go to bed.

"How's Tommy?" asked Evelyn.

"Not very good," said Herb tiredly. "The worst of it is, Evelyn, he's not a believer at all. He is so *hard*, for a young boy. He seems so completely indifferent."

"He's been through a lot," said Evelyn. "With all the operations he's had, and the illnesses."

"Well, it certainly hasn't softened him," Herb said sadly. "And if that kid doesn't pick up — I may have two funerals this week."

\*    \*    \*

Wednesday was a busy day. Herb made another trip in to the hospital, and was overjoyed to find that Tommy Evans was somewhat improved. He was home by 2:00. Evelyn left Donn with him and went shopping. Mainly to get away, she told him, smiling somewhat sadly. Not that she had much money to spend! She was going with the neighbor, Debby's mother, so it promised her a few hours of peace away from the strain of the parsonage.

He couldn't work at the church because he knew the church secretary would be there, typing and running the Sunday bulletins, and it just wouldn't be at all proper for him and Mrs. Armerding to be in the church alone — that is, "alone" together. Of course, Mrs. Armerding was ten years his senior, rather buxom, graying slightly, and anything but the village man-chaser. But one just couldn't be too careful, Herb knew. He had heard tales of alleged romancing between the pastor and various members of their congregations. Whether or not the stories were true, imagined, or told with malicious intent, really did not matter in the long run, Herb thought. If a man's ministry was wrecked at the outset because of indiscretion in this area, it certainly did no one any good whatsoever. So he carefully stayed away from the church Wednesdays during the hours from 2:00 in the afternoon until 4:30.

He had a couple of books which had been given to him by one of his church members and he decided to try to divert his mind from the funeral and all that went with it. Prayer meeting was tonight but he had already prepared for that. He settled himself down in his special chair with *Christ — Myth or Reality* and soon found himself fascinated by the author's brilliant defense of the Christian faith. With Donn curled up beside him part of the time he became lost in the pages of the book and was startled to hear the door opening.

Evelyn burst into the room, a package clutched under her arm. "Darling! A sale! Look. A new dress. *A new dress.* It was on sale. It's beautiful. I love it."

"And I won't even ask how much," said Herb. He watched while she opened the box and drew out a dress of fall colors blended in a modern print. "It really is beautiful," he added.

A pleased look came across her face and she held it up to her and paraded before him. "The other day while you and Donn were sleeping under the oak tree there by the Bay, I was day-dreaming about buying two new dresses for fall, one for good and one for all the time."

"Which is this?" he asked.

"This is for all the time," she said.

The telephone rang. It was Mina Thorpe. "Are we having prayer meeting tonight?"

"Of course," said Evelyn with a little laugh. "Why not?"

"Well, I just thought . . . with all the publicity and the funeral tomorrow, and everything, maybe. . . ."

"Seven-thirty as usual," said Evelyn. She hung up the phone and turned to face Herb indignantly. "Honestly!" All the joy had fled from her face. A tiny frown appeared between her eyes.

"Who was it?"

"Mina Thorpe."

"Figures." Herb wasn't really sold on the Thorpes,

who were a rather odd pair, to his thinking. Almost always the first ones to get up and give a testimony in a testimony meeting they were, nonetheless, far from what Herb thought of as dedicated Christians. Still, they kept the outward appearance of dedication, rarely missed a Sunday service or prayer meeting, and also most of the other church functions. He dismissed them with a sniff.

"What's for supper?"

"Eggs," said Evelyn, laying the dress over the arm of the chair gently. "Scrambled eggs, toast and coffee."

"Sounds like breakfast," said Herb, but he was content. His stomach just hadn't been the same since Monday, and he was nervous over the funeral tomorrow. He was concerned over the possible publicity at the event the next day, and would be greatly relieved when it was all over.

The Wednesday night service was well attended as usual. Herb had planned a missionary program for the evening, and had asked several of his members to investigate missionary possibilities in their own town and in Bayview, pointing out that "missions" was everywhere people were. He was gratified to hear the reports from those he had asked to report. Arthur Jennings, one of the staunch members of the church, had been asked to investigate the possibilities of the rest homes in the area. He had a rather grim report, as he had found that there were five rest homes in the area and that a great many of the people in the homes were seldom visited by relatives. He found they were indeed in need of a great many things spiritual and physical. There was real interest in the report.

Donna Carmichael had investigated the possibilities of a hospital visitation program. She had found there were two hospitals in Bayview that would allow church visitors if they got permission from the hospital first, and if they were appointed by the church as regular visitors.

Larry O'Neil, one of the six deacons, had investigated the west side of Bayview and the adjoining area, and found one place in the semi-slum area where there was no church for a space of ten blocks. He suggested that, perhaps with one of the other Baptist churches in Bayview, they could begin a cooperative Sunday school, with each church contributing a few members for the Sunday school hour.

"I might say," said Larry O'Neil, just before he finished his report and sat down, "that I was also in the area of Blueberry Drive and Ashton. That is really a needy area there, and I don't mean just needing the Gospel. We already have contact with one family in that area there, as you well know." He paused. "Events like what happened Monday just stress the desperate situation we are in today. Children are not safe on our streets and highways any longer. Unless we begin to penetrate the evil outside our church with the Gospel, we won't dare walk anywhere, anymore."

There was a murmur from the assembled men, women and children. Some of the mothers instinctively clutched their little ones to them protectively.

Herb stood up and thanked those who had given the reports. "You can see there is no room for slacking off the Lord's work," he said. "We have heard plenty tonight, and these are all things in which we can become involved as a church in the community. It is prayer time now. Remember me please, as tomorrow will be a very difficult day. And pray for the Ames family. They need Christ."

After the prayer service, several persons came up to him and expressed their anguish.

"Pastor Tabor, what is this world coming to?" asked Ben Thorpe. He was very pale, and visibly moved. The oldest Thorpe girl was with him and his arm was about her tightly. "It says it will be this way in the end times, doesn't it?"

"That's right," replied Herb. "Of course, things like this have been going on in the world since the beginning, too."

"But there's more of it today," insisted Thorpe. He looked really worn. "I've hardly slept since Monday, thinking if that had been Dawna, here. And that poor little kid. Imagine. Just killed and dumped in those weeds and dirt.

Why — it might have been Dawna!" His voice quivered, broke.

Herb looked at the girl, a child about twelve. Her eyes were wide and scared looking. She looked as though she hadn't had much sleep since Monday, either. Remembering the phone call they had received earlier in the afternoon from Mrs. Thorpe, Herb thought the whole family must be considerably shaken. They were a nervous bunch anyway, he knew.

Jim Carmichael stepped up at that moment and put out his hand. "Sorry about that piece in the paper, pastor," he said. "A lot of foolishness, of course, My wife and I know where you were on Monday morning at 9:00. And we'll tell everybody so, if need be." He reached out and took Herb by the shoulder. "We're praying for you," he assured him.

Others came up, some nervous and apprehensive, but none so much so as the Thorpes or Carl Johnson. Johnson came, looking anxious also. "Pastor, sorry to hear about the Ames girl. Terrible things happening these days. One wonders who is safe anymore. We'll be remembering you in prayer." He wrung Herb's hand anxiously. Herb thought Johnson looked rather pale also. And he was a little amused or touched at the man's "we," as his wife had been gone for two years.

*Thank goodness,* thought Herb later. *Some of the people can express themselves without getting maudlin about it.*

By 9:30 the church doors were locked and everyone had gone home. Prayer meeting was over.

The Tabors went to bed early in order to be rested for the ordeal the next day.

# 4

THURSDAY AFTERNOON CAME after a morning filled with telephone calls, last minute, hurried plans, and arrangements with a babysitter for Donn (Mrs. Gale obliged).

Herb sat looking out over the assembled people in the church with an outward appearance of tranquillity he did not feel. The Ameses looked worn and devastated, but calm. Seemingly they had weathered the terrible shock well. Ursula Ames actually looked better than he had ever seen her, Herb thought. She was dry-eyed, although her hand was clenched tightly around a handkerchief.

Behind the improvised screen of flowers Sandy Jones sat nervously, in full view of Herb, looking at him beseechingly. He flashed her a smile that was meant to be reassuring, but Sandy caught his tension, and forgot her own fears in her concern for her pastor.

Sally lay at the front of the church in a blue-gray casket with a pink rose spray, and Herb carefully kept his eyes turned in other directions for fear that, if he looked directly at her, he would become too emotion-choked to speak.

The organ stopped playing, and Herb arose to offer a prayer and to read Scripture. The Scripture he had chosen was the one which Evelyn had mentioned two days before . . . Psalm 116, the first fifteen verses. Herb read the verses slowly:

> I love the Lord, because he hath heard my voice and my supplications. Because he hath inclined his ear unto me, therefore will I call upon him as long as I live. The sorrows of death compassed me, and the pains of hell gat hold upon me: I found trouble and sorrow. Then called I upon the name of the Lord; O Lord, I beseech thee, deliver my soul. Gracious is the Lord, and righteous: yea, our God is merciful. The Lord preserveth the simple. I was brought low, and he helped me. Return unto thy rest, O my soul; for the Lord hath dealt bountifully with thee. For thou hast delivered my soul from death, mine eyes from tears, and my feet from falling. I will walk before the Lord in the land of the living. I believed, therefore have I spoken: I was greatly afflicted: I said in my haste, All men are liars. What shall I render unto the Lord for all his benefits toward me? I will take the cup of salvation, and call upon the name of the Lord. I will pay my vows unto the Lord now in the presence of all his people. Precious in the sight of the Lord is the death of his saints.

It seemed to Herb as though the Scripture fell into a hallowed place, as though it had been written for this specific occasion. He could hear subdued sniffing, and the dry, embarrassed cough of men who wanted everyone to know they were nonchalant and uncaring.

"I was brought low and he helped. . . . I will walk before the Lord in the land of the living. . . . Precious in the sight of the Lord is the death of his saints." It seemed that the last words, especially, hung in the air after they were spoken.

Immediately at the end of the reading came the soft voice of Sandy Jones singing:

> Jesus loves me, this I know
> For the Bible tells me so.
> Little ones to Him belong,
> We are weak, but He is strong.
> Jesus loves me, He will stay

Close beside me all the way.
Thou hast bled and died for me,
I will henceforth live for thee.
Yes, Jesus loves me; yes, Jesus loves me,
Yes, Jesus loves me — the Bible tells me so.

As the first words of the old song permeated the tense atmosphere of the church, people began to reach for their handkerchiefs and there was a prolonged nose-blowing session. But the soloist proceeded to the end without a quaver. Herb guessed she must be experiencing some special kind of strength, even as he was. As the song ended he arose to deliver his funeral message.

"We have come here today to pay tribute to a little girl who has passed suddenly from the scene around us. A little girl who was well known to us, who walked among us, and whose faith blessed our lives. I can tell you something about this girl that perhaps some of you do not know. The Psalm that was read can certainly be the testimony of Sally Ames.

"On the morning of the day that Sally Ames died, I gave her a ride to school after she had returned home to get her geography book. She told me something that I want to share with you, because it has come to mean much to me these past three days. As we were riding along, Sally said to me, 'You know, Mr. Tabor, yesterday you said that God always looks after us and cares for us. I *know* He does. I know Jesus loves me, because now I'm not afraid anymore. I used to be afraid, but not now. Not since last June.' I said then to Sally, 'That's wonderful to hear. That's the kind of news I need to make my day great. The Lord is with us, indeed, in all circumstances, and there is nothing that can harm us outside His will.'

"Little did I know that the words I spoke would come back to haunt me a few hours later. They *have* haunted me. It is no easy thing to bring this message today. But I still believe the Lord is with us in all circumstances, and there is nothing that can harm us outside His will. For us, Sally Ames has died, and we see her here as one who is lifeless and still. But Sally Ames is very much alive — more alive than she has ever been. I am convinced that God Himself ushered Sally into His presence. For Sally Ames, eternal life began the day she experienced true faith in Jesus Christ. That life has not stopped; it has taken on a new dimension, a dimension you and I do not know about . . . but Sally does. No matter how we die — whether it be lingeringly on a sickbed, or suddenly in a split second, to die in the body is to be present with the Lord. Of course we will miss her sunny face and her sweet voice, and her sturdy character . . . but heaven has gained a new citizen. Let us not then weep in mourning, but rejoice. We do not know the mind of God, but we know He makes no mistakes.''

Herb could not recall the entire message which he spoke, but he was conscious of strained, pale faces staring back at him from the pews . . . anxious faces, fearful faces, agreeing faces, even angry faces. Before he closed with prayer, he saw in the back row, almost hidden from his view under the shadow of the balcony, Officer Bailey from Homicide. Leaving no stone unturned, Herb thought. At least they were doing their job.

At last the service was over; it had lasted only thirty minutes, but it seemed interminable to Herb. Then there was the solemn wait while the family bid their last farewell to the departed one, and then the seemingly endless drive to the cemetery which actually was not far from the church.

Herb had thought a great deal about the words he would use when this moment had come. It was the final — the most devastating of all. Sad enough it was to have the body of your beloved one lying in view cold and unresponsive at the funeral parlor. But this — it was the end. No more able to even gaze upon the image of what had been.

He closed his eyes. ''Jesus said, I am the resurrection, and the life. . . . Whosoever liveth and believeth in me, though he were dead, yet shall he live. And whosoever liveth and believeth in me shall never die. Believest thou this?'' The words hung in the autumn air, hovered and dissipated slowly. The funeral was over. Herb stood back and watched some of the people as they murmured kind words to the family. There were not many relatives. A few neighbors had come and several from the church. Sally's class was there en masse.

The only thing of note that occurred was that Sally's teacher broke into violent sobs as they turned to leave the graveside. She was only a young teacher and had meant well. How could she have dreamed that such an innocent mission would turn into tragedy? A fellow teacher comforted her and the children looked embarrassed and uneasy. Relatives and friends moved over to the Ameses making futile attempts to say what was not sayable.

Herb heard a voice at his elbow. "That was a good message, preacher. You even believe it, don't you?"

Herb turned and saw the sturdy form of Lieutenant Bailey.

"Yes, I do," he responded with a positive note in his voice. "It is all that makes any of this at all bearable."

Bailey nodded. "I'll be dropping by to see you again in a day or so. We aren't getting anywhere, yet."

Herb nodded, hoping that his sudden panic did not show. "Anything I can do, Lieutenant," he said. Evelyn came up to him then, and together they left the cemetery.

"Let's take the long way home," she suggested. "I need to see some of God's beauty again."

Herb nodded. He felt that way himself. Both he and Evelyn enjoyed just driving, and both loved the out-of-doors, so he turned off onto a side road where trees lined the roadway on both sides to form a leafy canopy. "This will be gorgeous in a couple more weeks," he said. "We'll have to try and take a day off and sight-see."

She nodded, and came closer to him. "I was proud of you today," she said. "What you said had so much meaning. So many of us don't really believe what we say or do. But *you* do, don't you, honey?"

"Think I might get you converted after awhile?" he grinned at her.

"Rededicated," she said.

Supper was brief — hot dogs, potato salad, cole slaw, and coconut cream pie, Herb's favorite.

They had retrieved Donn from Mrs. Gale's capable hands, and at 7:00 they had both children in bed. They always tried to have the children in bed early enough to leave themselves some time for privacy each night. So far, it had worked. Now, at 7:00, as they were relaxing with the stereo and trying to forget the hardship of the past few days, the telephone rang.

It was Mrs. Ames. "Are you busy?" she asked, somewhat hesitantly. Evelyn assured her they were not. "Are you too tired to see us?"

"Not at all," said Evelyn matter-of-factly, but her heart leaped.

"We'll drive over in a little bit, then," said Mrs. Ames.

"Herb," breathed Evelyn, as she put the phone back on the hook. "You'll never guess . . . the Ameses . . . they're coming here."

*"What?"*

"They're coming over to see us," repeated Evelyn, her eyes shining. "Do you suppose . . . ? Let's see," she said automatically, "what can I serve them . . . maybe they just want to talk. Maybe. . . ." Her words trailed off as she vanished into the kitchen to see what goodies she had on hand.

Before she had really decided what to have, there was the ring of the doorbell, and Herb went to the door. "They're here," he reported, grinning. He turned the stereo down and then opened the door.

"Well, hello there," he said quietly. "How nice to have you come over. Come on in."

The couple entered and stood uncertainly in the space just inside the door. It was a warm night, and they had no jackets or sweaters. They still had on their "funeral clothes."

"Sit down," said Herb and Evelyn together. They placed their uneasy guests in comfortable chairs on a darkened side of the room.

There was a moment of silence, as Herb wanted a moment to analyze the situation and assess the needs of his callers. He was certain the call was not a social one. He did not have to wait long. With the same forthrightness exhibited by her daughter, Sally, Ursula Ames came quickly to the point.

"We know you're tired, Mr. Tabor," she said. "And we . . . we're tired, too." As though to verify this, she passed her hand wearily through her hair. "Never was there such a week. I've been a wreck. If it wasn't for that doctor and his nerve pills, I'd have never made it."

"Wonderful things, aren't they?" responded Herb, smiling at her. "Don't you ever wonder what people did before there were any tranquilizers?"

"I know what I would have done . . ." she said. "I'd have killed myself!" Her bitter, shocking words fell into a deep, startled silence. "I have nothing to live for," she went on. "Nobody really needed me, I thought. So I drank . . . and I've run around, a little." Her words ceased. Herb looked at John Ames. He realized the man was still sober.

"Ursie's always been runnin' from sumthin'," Ames said.

She looked at him. It was a long look, so long that Herb heard Evelyn take a deep breath. He found he was holding his. He let it out soundlessly.

"Why'n't you tell me that a long time ago?" Ursula Ames asked.

"You wouldn't have listened to me if I had," replied her husband.

She turned to Herb. "I been running from myself," she said. "I always hated me, even when I was a kid. I was always dumb — never could say anything right. I was clumsy. Soon as I was old enough, even before I was old enough, I guess, I started smoking. Then I started to take a drink, now and then. And then. . . ." Her voice faded again, and she looked down at the floor. "I can't live without it," she said.

There was another silence. Then her words started again. "When Sally was killed on Monday," she said, "it was just like I woke up, all of a sudden. You know I didn't treat her very nice. . . ." She bit her lip. Her voice sank to a whisper. "I treated her like a dog," she finished.

"Now, Ursie," said the man. "It wasn't all that bad. Sure, you used to bawl her out, and yank her around once in a while, but she knew you loved her."

"No — she didn't!" Her voice rose sharply, and the agony in it wrenched the room apart. "She *didn't*. That's what I can't stand. If only I could make it up to her!" She shed no tears, but she was trembling, Herb saw.

"What we came for, tonight," said Mr. Ames, turning to Herb, "was that today you said . . . you spoke so sure . . . you said Sally is alive. More alive than she has ever been. What d'ya mean?"

"I meant," said Herb, looking John Ames straight in the eye, "that your daughter asked Jesus Christ to come into her life last June. That means that beginning with that day, she has had eternal life, and can never die in the true sense of the word."

John Ames dropped his gaze to the floor. "I never had much truck with religious stuff," he said. "Never figured I needed it."

"Well, are you happy without it?" asked Herb, quietly.

There was another silence, after which he heard one word, almost inaudible. "No."

"Didn't it ever seem to you that Sally was somehow different the past few months?" asked Herb.

"She sang a lot around the house," said her father. "She used to sing 'Jesus Loves Me.' "

"Do you think He did?" asked Herb, stabbing mercilessly at the man.

"*You* said He did," replied Ames. He straightened up and squared his shoulders. "I don't see how you can make that fit with . . . what happened."

"Mr. Ames," said Herb, never taking his eyes from those of the man before him. "God has many ways of doing things which are strange to us, but He always has a reason. As for what happened, the first two days were torment for me; it seemed as though I couldn't reconcile it with what I thought God to be, and what He had allowed to happen. But my wife

73

solved that for me one night, in trying to answer our little girl. After all, to be with the Lord is our greatest joy; Sally is with Him now. What more could we ask?''

"Well, I suppose if you put it like that. . . ." John Ames' voice trailed off uncertainly. "I know Sally talked a lot about heaven, what it was like — how nice it would be to see the Lord. I never paid much attention to it. People always get all excited about it — when they first get religion. Then, after a while they're afraid of dying, just like everyone else. What I mean is," he amplified, spreading both hands wide and shrugging his shoulders, "heaven is real nice to talk about — but who wants to go right now?"

Herb smiled wryly. "None of us actually wants to go 'right now,'" he admitted. "But we never know when we might. That's why it is so good to see a person who is ready to go, if God takes him."

"What's ready to go?" asked John Ames. "I'm sure I ain't ready."

"Would you like to be?" Herb shot it at him.

"Ye . . es, I would," answered Ames slowly, but positively.

With hands that trembled slightly with excitement and joy, Herb pulled his Bible from the table and talked to Ames about sin, about God's love for men in Christ and what he, John Ames, needed to do about it. A few moments later, Ames slid to his knees in front of the chair; Herb followed suit, and while Ursula Ames looked on, wide-eyed and unbelieving, her husband prayed his first adult prayer, in a voice that was husky and strained. It was a short prayer, but to the point.

"God," he said, "I sure don't know what it's all about. But I know I sure am a sinner. I need what this preacher boy's got, and what my Sally had, and it's You that has to give it to me. I want Jesus Christ to . . . to live in me. Amen."

Evelyn could not see for tears; Ursula Ames looked white and miserable. "Now we're farther apart than ever," she said as her husband arose and sat down in the chair. "I never did understand you, John Ames. One minute you're

74

cussin' and drinkin' and now you've gone and got religion.''

"I quit drinking the day Sally was killed," answered Ames. He didn't turn to look at her; he was still too shaken to look around. He sat in the green chair with the tall back, and he leaned back in it. "I feel clean," he stated.

"You *are* clean," replied Herb.

"Was that all you wanted to see us about?" asked Herb. He was terribly happy about the husband's decision, but disappointed that the woman was not outwardly moved toward a decision for herself. It was by now 8:00, and Evelyn had gotten up and moved into the kitchen, wiping her eyes.

"I . . . guess so," said Ursula Ames. She did not look at him, but studied her fingernails, which gleamed blood red. She twisted her wedding ring around and around on her finger. She made a grab at her purse, and started to open it, but apparently thought better of that and put it down again, unopened.

Evelyn reappeared, bearing punch and sandwiches. She had gotten her prettiest dishes; Mrs. Ames looked impressed.

"These sure are pretty dishes," she said. "I oughta get new ones. If I start working again, that is."

"Oh, aren't you working any more?" asked Evelyn in surprise.

"No. I quit the day Sally was killed," she said. It was an echo of what her husband had said earlier. "There was that thing in the paper — about me working. I got the other two kids to think of, too."

Herb nodded. "It's a shame when mothers have to work," he agreed.

"Well," remarked John Ames in a low voice, "I ought to be able to work more, now that I ain't drinking."

"I can get a job at the dry cleaners, in Anchorville," said Ursula Ames. "Part-time. They told me I could." She put down her empty glass and plate suddenly. "We gotta go, John. Angela has to get the train back in the morning, you know." She stood up and, picking up her purse, moved toward the door.

John Ames heaved himself out of the green chair and

stood up straight. "I'm a new man," he said to Herb and Evelyn. "Never felt like this before. Can't wait to get to work tomorrow and tell my boss. He won't believe it."

Ursula Ames stood nervously by the door, looking miserable.

"It was wonderful that you came tonight," said Evelyn, taking her hand. "And . . . Mrs. Ames, don't you think *you* need Christ, too?"

"Yes — yes, I do!" cried the woman desperately. "I can't stand it if I don't have Him. Ever since you were there on Monday, Pastor Tabor, and told me what Sally said about how she wasn't afraid anymore, I've wanted to tell you. But I was afraid John would make fun of me." Tears fell swiftly from her eyes, down pale cheeks and onto her hands. Evelyn led her back into the room and she sat down in the chair again.

Herb picked up his Bible again, then stopped. "It's really no use going over all that again," he said. "You heard everything I said to John, Mrs. Ames. You know that you are a sinner and that Christ died to give you eternal life. A new life. Is that what you want?"

"Yes, oh, yes," whispered Ursula Ames. Like her husband, she slid out of the chair and onto her knees. "Lord, I'm an awful, wicked woman," she said. "I've broken every law You ever made. I mistreated my little girl until You had to take her away from me before I would know what I was doing. My little girl didn't know that I loved her, Lord. Please . . . please tell her for me, if You will. I'm going to be a new mother, God. I'm going to tell my kids about Jesus. If you'll make me new, God, like You did John."

The room had become a sanctuary; God was there. The four persons in the room sensed it. Never before had Herb and Evelyn felt so close to Him. He seemed to permeate every corner of the room and every corner of their hearts. It was like going to heaven for a few moments.

They were reluctant to arise, this time, but after a few long moments, Herb stood up. The feelings that he had were so violent and so real that it was as though he was being torn apart. He knew that in those brief moments they had come face to face with God; God was real. He was there, and Herb felt that, if it had been demanded of him, he could have put out a hand and pushed away a mountain.

In a few minutes the Ameses were gone. Herb and Evelyn rushed into each other's arms and wept and laughed together. "I feel as though I'm drunk," said Evelyn. "It's awful to say, or think, but Herb . . . Herb . . . God really *did* take Sally Ames home for a reason. Isn't it wonderful? We applied our faith, and said it was so. And it *is* so!"

"How happy Sally must be tonight, in heaven," said Herb. "Do you suppose He let her watch?"

"I'm sure of it," said Evelyn positively.

\*     \*     \*

Friday dawned, or rather erupted, a flaming sunrise over the bay. Recalling the old adage, "Red sky in the morning, sailor take warning," Herb cast an eye to the sky at 10:30, but there were no clouds. "It'll be a good day to get out the storm windows and wash them and put them up," he told Evelyn. "Suppose I get them out and you wash them, while I run to the hospital to see Tommy Evans. He was some better yesterday, but still isn't good. Then, when I get back from the hospital, I can put the windows on."

"Sounds great," said Evelyn. "Nothing I like better to do than to wash storm windows."

"Well, I know," said Herb, squirming beneath her steady gaze. "But it's such a nice day, and who knows but what it will rain tomorrow?"

"Besides, tomorrow is the young people's outing at Slippery Rock."

Herb groaned. "Oh, no. I forgot. Do I have to go?" he asked, looking at her pleadingly. It had been a hard week and the outing didn't sound good at all.

"I can't imagine why," Evelyn said mischievously. "But the young people always seem to want you there, even though they love the Joneses."

"But I'm so tired," protested Herb. "And I've got to study for Sunday's sermons."

"Yeah, yeah," said Evelyn, showing no sympathy whatever. "When you get the windows out, I'll wash them."

Herb got out the tall ladder from the church basement and got out the storm windows. Then he put the ladder up against the side of the house and started to wash the upper windows, knowing Evelyn wouldn't want to climb that high.

It was amazing what he could see from the top of the ladder, he thought whimsically, as he stopped washing for a moment and gazed around the streets of Anchorville. Trees blocked his view to the south, but to the west he could see Main Street, and the small shopping section that was open at the end. He could see almost the entire length of Fourth Street. He could see Mrs. Arnheim mowing her lawn with a hand mower. He could hear its soft clatter. He could see part of the school yard of the elementary school on Main and Third. It was recess time and children were out in the yard. Faintly, their shrieks and shouts drifted up to him. Across from the school, on the opposite side of Main, Herb could see a car parked. From that distance he could not tell the make of it, nor even guess why his eyes lingered on it.

Herb turned back to the window and washed the upper pane. He heard the schoolbell ring for classes to begin, and turned again to watch the children streaming into the building. He watched them go in, wondering if he could spot Pam in her red dress, and trying to imagine that he could. And then, as the last child entered the building, and quiet reigned once more, he saw the dark-colored car pull away from the curb and drive slowly out of sight, behind the trees which lined the Main Street.

Herb didn't think much about the incident, but his mind recorded it. He finished the upper house windows and brought the storm windows out where Evelyn could wash them easily.

Then he went in, changed his clothes, and drove in to Bayview to the hospital to see Tommy Evans, telling Evelyn he would be home in time for lunch.

*　　*　　*

Left alone, Evelyn got out fresh water and ammonia and a couple of clean, soft cloths. She washed the lower windows first and dried them, and then she washed the storm windows. Then she decided she could put up the storm windows on the lower part of the house by herself. So far, at least, she thought, it was a beautiful day. It was unseasonably warm, she realized, as she polished and as she put the windows into place, but there were still no clouds in the sky. Her mind, as she worked, was taken up with the incidents of the night before . . . Ursula Ames and her sudden capitulation to the Lord. The sight of the Ameses as they had gone out of the house the night before, close together and smiling, a little fearful after their experience of faith.

As for herself, Evelyn knew, her Christian life would never again be the same. After experiencing the nearness of the Lord the night before, even His sky looked different to her today. She wanted to rush up to each chrysanthemum plant spreading before her in the garden, to bury her nose in the blossoms, and to tell God over and over what a beautiful world He had made.

Donn played happily in the sand box, holding up fistfuls of sand and letting them trickle down over his clean, blue corduroy overalls. Even this didn't bother Evelyn today. As she washed and wiped, she prayed, sometimes soundlessly, sometimes softly aloud, for all the things she could think of that needed prayer: Herb, as he went to the hospital to see the rebellious little boy. Pamela, as she went to school and was sometimes pushed around by some of the other children — who didn't happen to like "preacher's kids." For herself, that she might be a better wife and mother. For the Ameses that they might grow and grow as Christians now, and that many lives might be changed because theirs had been. That they would find the murderer of Sally Ames.

She finished the windows and put away her cleaning equipment. Lighthearted and loving, she went into the house to fix lunch for Donn and Herb.

79

\*     \*     \*

The murderer drove around the block several times, each time seeming to battle the demon living within him. But he knew he would lose the battle. He wasn't even sure that he wanted to win it. He had had a small taste of excitement and power the other day — it was the urge to kill and the other urge that seemed to flood his whole being until he was one burning stick of unexploded dynamite. All that was needed now to light the fuse was the sight of the children at recess at Anchorville Elementary. There were no houses at that end of the block, and he pulled over to the curb and shut off the motor. His car started well; he could ignite his engine at any time. But he was getting crafty. He drew out a map from the glove compartment and pretended to be studying it. Actually, he looked beyond it — at the children. Several girls had come to a corner of the playground and were jumping rope. Four of them, there were. All healthy, happy children with hair and dresses flying. The murderer put down his map and started the motor, then he got out and pretended to check the tires. None of the girls looked over at him. They continued their merry game. Then the recess bell rang, and they ran, trailing the jump rope and calling to each other. "I'm first at noon!" "I'm second!"

The man got back into his car and drove slowly away with fire in his heart. He began to formulate some plan, some means, some excuse, whereby he might return to this spot at another hour. Another time. He could pretend illness — and indeed, that would not be too farfetched, he decided. He did feel ill; he was shaking with chills, yet he seemed to burn with a fever that was all-consuming.

He had been thwarted on Monday; he still could not understand why the child had expired so suddenly. Now, he was determined to be satiated. As he drove slowly off, his mind whirled in a turmoil, planning how he could return. It would be dangerous, it was true. Yet there was an element of excitement and anticipation that would not have been there if he had not been aware of the danger of the moment. He turned over in his mind the thought that he could stop off at the cemetery where Sally Ames was buried. He discarded this idea after toying with it for a minute, because he knew there was a chance the police would be there, waiting for that very thing — the return of the murderer.

Glancing at his wrist watch, he decided he had best linger no longer, but had better be on his way to work. Reluctantly he turned his car toward that destination.

# 5

I DON'T THINK YOU heard me," said Lieutenant Bailey to Herb, gruffly. "It is necessary that we know where you were yesterday between the hours of 12:00 noon and 4:00 in the afternoon."

Herb stared back at the officer and felt numbness stealing over him. "Well," he managed to bring out after a moment of concentrated thought, "I'm afraid I can't give you a very satisfactory answer to that, Lieutenant. First of all, I'm a minister so I have a variety of places to go and things to do. It's not that I do the same things consistently, day after day, like a person with a routine job. Yesterday . . . why, I helped my wife wash windows until, say, I don't know . . . 11:00, maybe. Then, I changed my clothes and drove to Bayview to see one of our church children who is in the hospital there."

"Anyone who can verify the time you were there?"

Lieutenant Bailey shot this at him so fast that Herb was completely dumbfounded. "Why — I suppose so, although I don't know. My wife saw me leave . . . she saw me come home. . . ."

"You were late getting home, remember?" Evelyn's voice cut into his sentence.

It was true. He had called her and told her he would be late. It had so happened that, after leaving the hospital, he had recalled he had to stop at a stationery or office supply store because the church's stationery supply was low, and he wanted to see about ordering some more. He hadn't been able to locate the office supply store right off and had driven around a bit before he found the place. Then, it had taken some time to get waited on and he had taken more time to pick out something he thought suited the church's image in the community. So he had called Evelyn, apologizing because he was going to be late for lunch, and, as a matter of fact, it had been quite late when he arrived home. It had happened that, at the post office in Bayview, he has encountered Ben Thorpe, who was mailing some packages for his company, and he had suddenly realized the man was looking rather seedy lately. Herb's impatience with the family had given away to pity, and he had listened patiently while Thorpe told him about his own liver condition and his wife's gall bladder. All this had taken time, and, as so often happened when there was no really specific thing to do, time had seemed to slip by quickly.

After that, Herb recalled, he had gone to downtown Bayview because he had remembered that he had seen a sweater in the window of one of the stores that looked to be a good match for the colors in Evelyn's new dress, and he intended to find out the price. If it was not too much, he had intended to somehow squeeze his budget to allow the purchase. Evelyn had so little, he thought, and she did so much for him — meant so much to him. It wasn't often that he bought her anything to wear. Candy, maybe, once in a while, and one time on their anniversary, a dozen roses. But they had been so especially close that week, and he wanted to give her something a little extra. As it turned out, the sweater had been too small and they did not have one in her size, so he had gone out again, somewhat frustrated, and had encountered another member of his flock on the sidewalk. He was surprised to see him, too, because the man was a truck driver and was usually out of town most of the week.

Ernest Rhodes had hailed him and had complimented him on the way he had handled the events of the week. "You're always there, pastor, when we need you," he said. "The last man we had here just never seemed to care about calling, and put everything into his sermons. Not that you don't preach good sermons," he added, and Herb realized that his too-expressive face must have given away the little flicker of annoyance he had felt.

For some reason or other, although Rhodes was a good deacon, a fine Christian as far as Herb knew, he had an unfortunate way of stating things. It was as though he had an inner compulsion to hurt, and this was kept in check due only to his stern repression of it most of the time.

Herb had talked to Rhodes for perhaps ten minutes, and then he had broken away, saying that he was already late for lunch. It had been close to two o'clock when he finally sat down to a warmed-over lunch.

Evelyn had been a little provoked with him because, as she had said, she had spent some time to prepare a lunch he liked especially well and he was late. She must be getting a little tense, he thought, because pettiness wasn't like her. Although, he had to admit, it wasn't much fun to fix lunch for someone if they didn't come to eat it! He had apologized handsomely and had been forgiven handsomely. All these things flashed through his mind now, while he sat thinking.

He stared back at Bailey and said somewhat brusquely, "Just why are you asking me these questions, Lieutenant?"

"Because," said Bailey somewhat painfully, "last night a little girl was reported missing from the Anchorville area, and they found her body this morning. The little girl had been criminally assaulted and strangled."

"Oh!" A long drawn breath from Evelyn. Herb could feel her eyes on his face. He was too shocked to speak. He could feel the blood leaving his face and there was sweat on his palms.

"I know nothing about it," he said finally, through stiff lips.

"I sure hope not," said Bailey. "You *look* like a nice guy. But — you can never tell nowadays."

"He *is* a nice guy," said Evelyn softly. "You don't know Herb. He wouldn't hurt a fly."

"Who was the girl?" asked Herb, hoping selfishly and fervently it would not turn out to be another member of his own congregation.

"Kathy Kwekel," said Bailey. "Pretty little girl. Eight years old. I had to go and tell her mother this morning. I don't like that kind of assignment."

"Where do they live?" asked Evelyn. "I don't recall the name at all."

"On Main and Argyle," said the officer. "Not very far from the school, actually. No one can remember for sure if she was there for the last recess in the afternoon, or whether she disappeared after school, on the way home. It could have gone either way."

"If you think she disappeared after afternoon recess, or after school, then why did you ask me where I was yesterday from 12:00 on?"

"Well, it's a funny thing," said Bailey, scratching gently over his right ear. "But no one can say positively at the school that she was there even earlier in the afternoon. Some say they saw her . . . others say she wasn't there. But, as it happens, Fridays they have a class in 'music appreciation' in the afternoon, and they have art classes . . . and that means that the kids aren't necessarily seated at one particular desk for the afternoon. They are more informal, it seems, and the children are allowed to move around some. Just one of those things."

"When was she reported missing?" Evelyn could not get past the shock of it. She could easily imagine what her own feelings would be if it became very late in the afternoon and Pammy had not come home.

"Actually not until about 5:00 last evening," said Bailey. "At first the mother said she thought the girl might have gone to a friend's house to visit for a while, so she didn't worry too much, although she did call a couple of places to see if the girl was there. But at 6:00 she was sure something was wrong, and she called our department. By seven we had about a hundred people out looking. Of course it gets dark quite early, now." He paused, turned his hat around and around in his two meaty hands. "We found her this morning," he said.

"I'm sorry," said Herb tonelessly. "If there is anything at all we can do . . . just let us know."

"They have their own church," said Bailey. "Thank you for your time," he added. He heaved his weighty bulk out of the chair and ambled toward the door.

"Wait!" Herb had suddenly remembered something — something that might help. "Yesterday," he said, "I was washing the upper windows on the house and I stopped for a minute and looked over the town — it's really surprising what you can see from the top of an eighteen or twenty foot ladder."

Bailey nodded, his eyes steady on Herb's.

"I could see all the way to the school — the schoolyard, that is," said Herb. "And it was morning recess time. I remember that, at the time I looked, the children were playing and there was a car parked on the side of the street across from the schoolyard."

"What color car?"

"A dark car — dark blue, dark green, or black," said Herb. He concentrated, trying to recall just what it had looked like.

"Was it a small car — a large car?"

"Well," said Herb cautiously, "I don't think it was anything unusual. It wasn't a sports model, a compact, or anything like that. It was just an ordinary, run-of-the-mill car, as I recall it."

"It's a lead, anyway," said Bailey without excitement. He took out a small, black notebook and wrote a few scribbles in it. "Did you see the car leave?"

Herb stretched back into his memory again. "Ye-es,"

he said slowly, trying to be exact. "As I recall it, the recess bell rang, and then this car pulled away."

Bailey looked at him sharply. "Buddy," he said softly, "if you're telling the truth, you've given us the first lead we've had in this case. And we need 'em." As he turned away they heard him say under his breath, "*if* you're telling the truth." The door was open and he loosed the catch on the screen door and went out, without looking back.

"Why wouldn't I be telling the truth?" Herb asked. Evelyn did not answer. Instead, she said:

"Herb, it's like a nightmare. Is this real? Is this us?"

"I'm beginning to ask myself the same thing," he said. This time he didn't try to comfort her; he went outside. He got into his car and drove off without knowing where he was headed. Had he looked behind him he would have seen that the officer had not left. As soon as Herb's car left the driveway Lieutenant Bailey's car followed behind discreetly.

Herb drove toward the bay road. Whenever he was hurt or troubled or tired he always headed for the bay. There was peace at the bay. He recalled that only Monday, he and Evelyn had driven out here with joy and had spent a beautiful afternoon. It was now only a dim memory. He drove as rapidly as he could on the winding road that led to Peaceful Point, as they called it, with their own, private name. Because of the turmoil within him, Herb scarcely noticed some of the red maples were turning. The miles passed swiftly.

Herb's concern was not now with himself, primarily, but he realized that, on Sunday, he would have to get up before his people and preach . . . and he didn't feel that he could possibly do it. On Monday he had formulated plans for a new topic for Sunday morning services; he had intended starting a study on the Book of Ephesians. The week had been so intensely full of events and out-of-the-ordinary occurrences that he had put off trying to prepare his sermon until Saturday. But that was today, and he had no song to sing — no sermon to preach.

The drive seemed short and, suddenly, he was there. It was all the same — the water was blue and mainly unruffled, leaves floated near the shore where sandpipers ran and sea gulls plodded along, or swooped and dipped over the water with their plaintive, mewing cries. Herb stopped the car and got out. He walked to the water's edge and found a spot on a large log, where he sat. Presently, as he stared out across the bay the turmoil of his thoughts stopped and his world began to swing back into focus. What a fool he was! He realized that he had gone off and left Evelyn to cope with everything for the afternoon while he ran like a dog with his tail between his legs. If God was real at all — and they had certainly met Him afresh this week — He could heal everything — make everything right. He was big enough so that Herb could trust Him.

Herb got to his feet and began to walk rapidly down the beach. As he walked, he talked to the Lord as was his custom. "Lord, I guess I'm only a dumb preacher," he said. The blood was flowing back into his face and his whole body felt alive now. "I'm really good at telling other people how to be good Christians, but I guess I can't take much, myself," he said further. "Lord, I don't know why You put up with such a poor specimen of a man as I am, but You called me to this work, and this must all be a part of Your plan for me. Give me faith, Lord. Give me faith. I pray for Sally's parents, Father, that they may come to know You better each day. And I pray, too, Father, for the parents of that other poor little girl. And, Lord, I even pray for the murderer — a man who is in danger of hell — a man who has killed two persons — taken two human lives, Father. Help him. And help the police to find him before he kills again. Bless my poor little wife, Lord. And Lord . . ." he paused. "Thank You for all You've given to us this week. For all the wonderful blessings we've had, even in the midst of all the trouble. Thank You for coming to earth in Your Son, for I ask all these things and thank You in His name."

A faint breeze wafted across the water at that moment, carrying a sweet scent of moisture and wild flowers. It was like a benediction.

Herb found that he had walked nearly a mile down the beach. He turned around and set off toward the car at a brisk pace, and in fifteen minutes was back in the car. He swung the blue Chevrolet around out of the parking place and headed back the way he had come.

Five hundred feet down the road the police car swung in behind him. This time Herb saw it . . . and understood. An hour before he would have sweated. Now a mischievous thought struck him and about three miles down the road, he suddenly pulled off to the side and waited for the officer to come up. He got out of his car and stopped Bailey.

"Just wanted to thank you for the escort," he said. Then he turned around and got back into his car, while Bailey's face turned a brick red.

*     *     *

The *Bayview Bugle* was in the hands of the citizens again. It did not have the outcome of the search, but the headlines screamed the news: CHILD MISSING: FEARED SLAIN BY KILLER. It read well, written by the eager hand of Timothy O'Leary.

> Second child missing in Anchorville since yesterday shortly after lunch. One hundred persons searching until after dark last night failed to turn up any trace of Kathy Kwekel, second child to disappear in Anchorville this week. The first child, Sally Ames, was slain in Bayview but came from Anchorville, where the second child also lives. Police and sheriff's deputies from both towns tried until 1:00 this morning to find anyone who recalled having seen the girl after 12:00 yesterday. Because of the varied programs on Fridays at Anchorville Elementary School, no one can say for sure if Kathy ever came to school after lunch. She was at school all morning, say school authorities, and went home for lunch at 12:00. Her mother says Kathy ate well and left for school again at 12:20 or 12:25, so she would have time to play on the school grounds before school started again.
>
> Kathy was wearing a blue and red plaid cotton dress when she was last seen by her mother, brown loafer shoes and white, knee-length stockings. She is blonde and was

wearing a red bow in her hair. Police in both Anchorville and Bayview will be glad to have calls from anyone who can give any information concerning the girl, who possibly may have seen her walking back to the school, or any one who recalls positively if she was at the school any time after lunchtime. Sheila Duggan and Pamela Waverly say they did not play with Kathy during the afternoon recess, or at lunch.

Folks in both towns are beginning to wonder if it is safe to let little girls walk anywhere by themselves anymore. Certainly, until the killer is apprehended, it is unwise for any parents to let their children walk to or from school alone. If at all possible, Police Chief Garber of the Bayview force says parents should form car pools to transport the children to the very doors of the school if necessary, to prevent a recurrence of this week's tragedy.

\*     \*     \*

On Sunday morning Herb got up to preach from Ephesians, the first chapter. After a considerable battle with himself and with the Lord, he had given in. He was now prepared. After the choir had sung and the offering had been taken, he arose and looked out over his congregation. It had not been depleted by the week's tragedy. If anything, there were more people. Some, he thought, had come no doubt out of simple curiosity. But at least two persons who looked up at him from the vantage point of one of the front pews, had not come out of curiosity. They had come because they had found new lives.

Ursula Ames was neat and subdued looking; John Ames looked pale but composed. The five-year-old Kelly sat between them, round eyed and sober. It was her first Sunday in church, and it was all new.

When the three had walked down the middle aisle and had taken their seats, John Ames sitting very properly to the side, there were incredulous looks from a dozen persons. And tears had come to the eyes of some when the bereaved parents walked in. It was a tremendous moment for Herb. He looked at Evelyn; their eyes locked, hers saying, "I love you, darling." Herb felt a wave of pure joy which simmered to a subdued sadness as he realized anew that there should ideally have been another face in the pew — that of Sally Ames. But in a sense she was there, the whole service.

Now, Herb found himself saying words that seemed to come from beyond himself, words he would not have chosen. He read from the first chapter of Ephesians slowly, the congregation responding by reading every other verse.

> Grace be to you, and peace, from God our Father, and from the Lord Jesus Christ. Blessed be the God and Father of our Lord Jesus Christ, who hath blessed us with all spiritual blessings in heavenly places in Christ: According as he hath chosen us in him before the foundation of the world, that we should be holy and without blame before him in love: Having predestinated us unto the adoption of children by Jesus Christ to himself, according to the good pleasure of his will.

"This has been the most difficult week of my life," he began. "Things have happened this week that have shaken us all — some more than others. We meet today, and one of our own has been taken out of our midst, God having promoted her to the reality of the 'heavenly places in Christ Jesus' that Paul speaks of in the second chapter of this wonderful letter which he wrote. And I'll be perfectly frank with you," he went on, "and say that I miss Sally Ames, because she was a bright spot in our midst. From the day of her conversion last June she bore a radiant testimony of her faith in Christ." Herb was conscious that his words were bringing tears to many, but he continued, knowing that the tears were good.

"I had planned to speak on Ephesians for the next few weeks, or possibly months, but for a while this week I didn't think I could bring myself to preach on this particular portion. But this morning I have a message from God — the same message that Paul brought to the church at Ephesus — a message of grace and peace."

Time flowed, people wept, and Herb preached as he had

91

never preached before. At the close of his sermon, he stepped forward and said, "Now it may be that there are some here today who have never made a public profession of their faith in the God who brought this message of grace and peace. If there are those here this morning who would do so, would you come and stand here with me at the front of the sanctuary, and let this congregation know that this very day you want to be a follower of Jesus Christ."

As the organist began to play, a man stood up and moved out of the pew in which he was sitting. Herb could feel tears on his face, as he stepped forward to meet John Ames. He looked back. Ursula Ames was standing with her head bowed, both hands clutching the pew so that her knuckles showed white. Herb could not speak. It was a moment that those who do not *know* can never understand. And through the blur that was in his eyes, he saw another figure slip out of a back pew and start up the aisle. It was Dawna Thorpe, the Thorpes' twelve-year-old daughter.

At last, when the organ had stopped playing and Herb was beginning to talk with Dawna Thorpe, and one of the deacons had taken John Ames into the prayer room, Ursula Ames relinquished her white-knuckled hold on the pew before her, and walked up to stand at the front of the church. She wept and the people in the pews wept and there was scarcely a dry eye in the entire church.

"Certainly God is here this morning," said Herb, taking advantage of the evident moving of the Spirit. "He is speaking to hearts all over the congregation. God takes some ways that are strange to us to bring us to Himself, but the coming is good. Perhaps there are those here this morning who are already members of this church, but who would like to rededicate their lives to be used of God in whatever ways He would."

Slowly, from here and there in the pews, people began to step out and come down the aisle, so that, after all her long battle with herself and with the Lord in making a "public confession" — a spectacle of herself as she had feared, Ursula Ames found herself surrounded by perhaps twenty persons who were as moved as she. Among those who had made a rededication of themselves that morning were three of the church's deacons — deacons who had been giving Herb a little trouble every now and then, thinking that perhaps he was too young to always know what he was doing. Arthur Jennings and his wife Anne came; Forrest and Peggy Thompson, and Ernest Rhodes.

To Herb, it seemed as though all the pains and scars of the past week had vanished and again he felt he could move mountains if need be. His own wife was one of those who came, and his own little daughter Pam, who whispered shyly that "she wanted Jesus to come into her heart, too."

It was anticlimactic; Herb felt suffocated, drained, as though he could rejoice, but weep no more.

\* \* \*

Monday morning came. Was it possible that only one week had elapsed since their wonderful picnic of last Monday? The whole week had passed at breakneck pace. Nor could it be said that things were back to normal. With Monday morning came another edition of the *Bayview Bugle* and another lengthy article from the pen of the ever-energetic O'Leary.

> Citizens of Bayview and Anchorville are sorrowing today. Another little girl lies in a Bayview funeral home and today will be carried out and laid to rest in the same cemetery where, just last Thursday, Sally Ames was buried. Two families are grieving this week because of a sudden, tragic loss . . . a loss that need never have been, if parents would prepare their children properly before sending them off to school, or to the store.
>
> Statistics tell us that the killers of little girls and boys usually pick them up first, with promises of candy or a treat, or the promise of seeing some new thing or other that would be appealing to the child. Proper home training, the experts say, would arm children with the simple weapon of refusal. Not too many older children are actually kidnapped as we think of the word; actually, they are

lured into cars with simple offers of goodies of one kind or another. All parents in Anchorville should prepare their children today to use a simple word: *no*.

Sad to say, the killers often are friends of the child's family, or, even worse — relatives. This is one reason why children will climb into a car and go so willingly with a child-molester. Sometimes it is a complete stranger; more often it is a man whom the child knows.

It is hoped that the police force of Bayview and Anchorville will speedily locate the killer of these two pretty little girls before he strikes again.

"At least he left me alone this time," said Herb thankfully, as he laid the paper down and looked at Evelyn. "But after yesterday, I don't think anything will ever bother me again. Of course," he added ruefully a moment later — "I didn't think it would after Thursday night, either, but it didn't take much to prick my big balloon."

"Yesterday was wonderful, wasn't it?" agreed Evelyn. Since it was Monday morning, she was wearing a casual outfit — a bright red, long-sleeved blouse, a faded blue denim skirt and a band around her hair. In this ancient and comfortable costume she felt she was ready for almost anything, outside of a luncheon engagement at the Ship House in Bayview. If need be, she had told Herb earlier, it was old enough so that she could even work in it — if she had to. But after all, it *was* Monday. And Monday was their "day off."

As so often happened at the parsonage, the telephone rang. Evelyn answered it and heard the hurried voice of Margaret (Peggy) Thompson at the other end.

"Are you and the pastor going to be home this afternoon?"

"Just a minute," said Evelyn, holding her hand over the phone. She turned to ask Herb, "Are we going to be home this afternoon? It's Margaret Thompson. Evidently she wants to see us about something."

A faint frown creased Herb's forehead as he heard this. He had been figuring a little on going for a drive somewhere — not the bay road, but in another direction, perhaps north, to enjoy the beauty of early-turning leaves. It was really early yet, and he realized he was probably thinking up excuses to get away.

"Ask her if she can wait," he told Evelyn.

"Mrs. Thompson?" asked Evelyn. "Is it something that can keep until tomorrow? Could you see us tomorrow?"

"Well . . . " the voice at the other end of the line faded out, came back again, stronger, but somehow breathless. "I really didn't think . . . I've been wanting. . . ."

Evelyn put her hand over the phone again. "I think it's something important," she whispered. "She sounds upset."

Herb made up his mind quickly. "Tell her of course we'll see her this afternoon," he said. "Any time."

"Mrs. Thompson," said Evelyn, trying to make her voice sound extra friendly and reassuring, "my husband says to tell you we'll see you this afternoon. How about two?"

"Oh! That will be fine. Wonderful!" The woman's voice changed instantly, became grateful, relieved. "I'll be there at two."

The Thompsons lived in Anchorville, not more than three blocks from the parsonage, so the woman would probably walk over, Evelyn thought. Well, there went the afternoon . . . as usual. A moment later, she repented of her self-pitying thoughts. After all, what were they there for? Why, for just such things as helping their members who were suffering from anxiety, problems of all sorts, griefs, joys. She smiled at Herb. "There'll be other afternoons," she said. "We can wait."

\*     \*     \*

The woman who sat in his study with him was extremely nervous, Herb could see. She was holding herself in rigidly, but her eyes held little darts of fear. . . . Herb could not imagine what Margaret Thompson could possibly be worried about. She was, ordinarily, the most genial and relaxed person imaginable. She was a so-called "pillar" of the church, a do-gooder who was always helping to bind up someone's wounds, physical or spiritual; a woman who could well have been the spiritual counterpart of Dorcas or Tabitha of the New Testament.

Now she sat across from Herb, and her hands were frantic. She kept placing them in her lap and pressing her fingers together to keep them still. But in a moment, one hand would be playing with her string of beads, or patting her hair, or stroking the other hand.

"My dear lady, what is it?" Herb asked finally, seeing that seemingly, she could not bring herself to speak.

At his words her pent-up emotion broke, and she said raggedly, "I just can't say it, Pastor Tabor, but I'm just frantic with fear." She put one hand over her lips, which were trembling.

"Yes?" encouraged Herb patiently.

"Do you think my husband would . . . kill someone?" The last words came out in a whisper, so soft that Herb had to strain to hear them. Yet he did hear them.

Shocked, silenced, he stared at her, uncomprehending.

"My dear lady," he said, repeating his former words.

"My doctor says I always imagine things too easily, and worry too much," Margaret Thompson said. "But Pastor Tabor . . . " She stopped again. "Ever since last Monday," she said, "I've just wondered and wondered."

"What happened on Monday?" Herb asked.

"Forrest came home ill Monday afternoon," she said. "He really *was* ill, too. And he's been so nervous, lately. He didn't used to be like that at all," she went on. "But lately, he has been so different. He is irritable, snaps at me so often — not like himself at all. I have just thought he was working too hard. They work so hard down at the plant, you know. And Forrest works overtime quite often. But Monday he came home early — at 3:30 in the afternoon. He said he had a headache, and he was a little nauseated, but that seemed to wear off, after a while. His headache went away, too."

"Sounds like he needs a good check-up," offered Herb. He was still so surprised he could scarcely think of anything intelligent enough to say.

"Yes," she agreed. "I've tried to get him to go to a doctor. But men . . . " she paused. "Men don't like to go to doctors very well, I guess." She paused, and stared at her hands a moment. They were still, finally, as though with the sharing of her burden she had released her pent-up fears.

"Well, but I still don't understand," said Herb. "Even if he did come home early, and if he was ill, whatever makes you feel that he is in any way connected with a killing?"

"Well," said Margaret Thompson, leaning forward a little. "I never did, of course. But we heard about it on the radio, you know, Sally Ames."

"Ah," said Herb, as though the idea had not occurred to him before. Actually, it had. From the very first, he had realized that here was a person who was not only fearful of her husband's actions, but she was fearful of a specific deed, namely, the murder of Sally Ames.

"My husband was listening to the report," she said, "and, oh! How can I talk about it?" She pressed her hand over her lips again. In a few seconds, she continued. "He fainted."

"Forrest?" said Herb incredulously. "He fainted?"

"Yes," said the woman. "He was sitting there with me and Bob . . . his brother Bob, you know . . . and we were watching the broadcast on television . . . and he just fainted. He just simply passed out cold. I couldn't rouse him. I was terrified. Of course, at the time I didn't think a thing about it, *but* . . . I said to Jack Vander Cook on Wednesday night at prayer meeting that I hoped Forrest was feeling better, and that I was sorry he had had to come home early on Monday. And — do you know what Jack said to me? This is what absolutely terrifies me. He looked at me so strangely, Pastor Tabor. And he said, 'Forrest didn't come to work at all on Monday. Wasn't he home?' " With the last words, she became silent.

Herb sat so still he could hear the small clock ticking on the bookcase in the corner. The world whirled a little, and then came back into focus. Thompson was one of his dependables. A real square, fine fellow. He had been one of the ones who had come forward on Sunday for rededication of his life. The idea that the man was anything he did not appear to be was absolutely preposterous, as far as Herb was concerned. Except, of course, the fact of his strange and inexplicable behavior.

"I'm shocked at what you told me," he said to Mrs. Thompson, "and of course I can offer no explanation for it all. But I would urge you to trust your husband. After all, you've been married a good number of years, and he has always been a good husband, has he not?"

"Oh, yes, Mr. Tabor!" cried Margaret Thompson. "Forrest and I have been married for nearly thirty years. We've had words, at times, of course, I guess that's healthy, according to the psychologists — but he has never kept anything from me, before."

"There are times when everyone keeps something back," Herb assured her. "Talk to the Lord about it; trust your husband, and I'm sure everything will be all right. I cannot believe such a thing of Forrest."

Still shaken in his own soul, he managed to comfort the agitated woman and had prayer with her before she left. By the time she walked out the door of the study she had managed a faint smile, and seemed to be feeling better for her interview.

Evelyn had sat in the church just outside the study during the conference as they had formed this as a system as soon as Herb had taken a church. For convention's sake they both felt that Evelyn should accompany him to the church study when the person being counseled was a woman. This measure was to preclude the start of any malicious gossip on the part of neighbors who might chance to see the pastor of the church going into the church with a woman — even if she were thirty years his senior. However, unless the person interviewed requested it, Evelyn did not accompany them into the study.

Now, as Mrs. Thompson walked out, she smiled at Evelyn, and thanked her for waiting outside. She walked as far as the side door, then turned and came back. "I know you gave up some afternoon plans for me,'' she said to them both, ''and I thank you.''

They were touched to think that she realized that they had given up something to see her, and the afternoon took on a warm glow, for Evelyn, at least.

Herb had no warm glow at all. The interview had done his church member good; it had done him evil. If (and there did seem to be a remote possibility at least that such could be the case) Forrest Thompson was indeed guilty of the murder of Sally Ames, then he, Herb Tabor, had become, as a lawyer would say, ''an accessory after the fact.'' For now he shared a guilty knowledge, if the man were guilty. But he could not go to the police very well without the permission of the woman herself, as he would be betraying a confidence. His own position as a suspect did not give him a good leverage for reporting such a thing. It would be nice for him if the police could turn up another suspect — but not Forrest Thompson!

Herb walked back to the parsonage with Evelyn, his chin sunk on his chest, in deep thought. She walked silently beside him until they reached their own back porch, then she spoke hesitatingly. ''Herb, you are really troubled. Can you tell me?''

Sunk in his own black thoughts he answered somewhat briefly. ''No, my dear, I'm sorry. But this is one time I can't tell you about it.'' He didn't want Evelyn to worry, for one thing. And the fewer persons who knew about it, the better.

Evelyn accepted it unquestioningly, he thought. He made no further reference to the visit, nor did she. But that afternoon marked the beginning of a tiny wedge between them, a wedge that came and was not even recognized by either of them until it had pressed in between them and caused a break in their close relationship.

# 6

TUESDAY MORNING at 8:30 Herb and Evelyn left to attend a meeting of their area association. The meeting was at Willow City, about forty miles away. They left Donn with Mrs. Gale, as Evelyn did not want the little fellow to have to sit through the all-day meeting with them.

It was a well-attended meeting and Herb met several fellow pastors from his own area. The 10:00 speaker was excellent. His sermon topic was taken from the twelfth chapter of the Book of Hebrews: "Wherefore, lift up the hands which hang down and the feeble knees . . ." "Too many weak-kneed Christians today," he thundered, "and not enough to work willingly with their hands at God's work." The speaker read the verse also from something he called a "Simplified New Testament":

> Therefore, up with your hands that are now dangling down, and make those weak knees of yours strong again! Keep your feet in straight paths so that if one is lame he may not be turned out of the way, but rather be improved.

Herb was impressed. He wondered where he could obtain the translation read. It certainly hit him between the eyes, he thought. "*Weak knees.*" Boy! That was the story of

Herb Tabor, all right. He squirmed a little in his seat, and Evelyn looked at him, a question in her eyes.

They had a good day; they saw some old friends there and met the former pastor of Grace Baptist Church. His name was Howard Dilson. They were glad to meet him, having heard good comments on his ministry from most of the church people. He was an older man, with a strong and good-humored face, and a shock of white hair that looked as luxuriant as that of a man twenty years his junior. Laughing creases marked his face at the corners of his eyes and mouth.

"I hear you've had some trouble over there, lately," he said after he had introduced himself. "I was terribly shocked to hear about the little Ames girl. I remember the family very well."

"There were some things that happened, though, that didn't get in the papers," Herb told him hurriedly. He told how the girl had been converted in June and how, after her funeral, the parents had come to make a confession of faith.

"Wonderful! Wonderful!" the older man beamed. "When you leave a place, you know, a little of you always stays behind. It is certainly good to hear of the blessing there, as well as the not-so-good news." He stood for a moment, deep in thought then raised his eyes again, looking questioningly at Herb. "Have they any idea of who might have killed her?"

"They have just one suspect," replied Herb somewhat drily. "And I'm it!"

The older man laughed loudly, then seemed to sense that Herb was serious. "You're joking, of course," he said hesitantly.

"No, really I'm not," said Herb. "One of the reasons we made a special effort to come today was because we greatly needed to get away . . . the telephone, you know. Besides, another girl was killed Friday."

"No!" It was an explosive, incredulous negative.

"I'm afraid it's so," said Herb. "And I wasn't home all the time during the possible hours of death." Seeing the unbelieving look on Dilson's face, he tried to explain further.

"You see, Mr. Dilson, I picked Sally Ames up and took her to school the day she was killed. It's really quite a long story. But I sure didn't know what I was getting into."

"Well, I should say not," replied Dilson. He breathed deeply, exhaling in a long sigh. Then he touched Herb lightly on the shoulder. "I'll be praying for you," he said. The P.A. system announced the next session and Dilson hurried off to join his wife. They did not see him again at the meeting. Late in the afternoon they drove home again, and picked up the children at the Gales' home.

Coming up their street, Evelyn gave a contented sigh. "It was a good, good day," she said. "It did me a lot of good."

"Me, too," agreed Herb. As he stopped the car in their own driveway, he stretched widely and yawned. "I guess I must have relaxed," he added. From the car they could hear the telephone ringing, and they looked at each other resignedly.

"I can't face it," said Evelyn crossly. "I hate it. I'm going to tear it out by the roots one of these days."

"Someone would just find it and plant it again," said Herb cutely. They laughed.

"Lemme out," squealed Donn. "Donn's hungry."

"Donn's always hungry," said Evelyn. "You take after your father." She put the boy down on the ground outside the car and leisurely got out herself, making no move to go into the house toward the ringing telephone. Donn ran to the edge of the drive and scooped up some sand. Pam ran around the house to get her hoola hoop.

"See?" said Evelyn. "It's stopped. I knew it would. It had to."

"You're a naughty girl," said Herb. "A good preacher's wife answers the telephone gladly, willingly, pleasantly and promptly."

"Well, that lets me out, then," said Evelyn. "Right this minute I'm being a bad preacher's wife."

They were at the front door when the telephone started to ring again. Reluctantly Herb speeded up his steps and crossed the short distance to the alcove in the living room where the second house phone rested in its cradle on the wall.

"Hello?" he said half-heartedly, taking up the receiver.

"Bailey here," snapped the voice at the other end of the line. "Where have you folks *been*, anyway? I thought preachers had to stay home always to answer the telephone."

"Preachers hardly ever stay home," retorted Herb. "And sometimes their wives like to get away, too." His tone was somewhat stiff. Something in the officer's tone irritated him right at that moment.

"I'd like to see you," Bailey said. "Right away."

"Don't tell me someone else has been killed," said Herb, unsympathetically. "At least, if they were, I'll have an alibi today. My wife went with me this time." It was sheer bravado; the minute Bailey said he wanted to talk with him, the churn began to turn in his stomach.

"We just had something turned in I thought you would like to see," said Bailey. "I'll be along in a few minutes."

"Why do you always come at supper time?" Herb asked the question without thinking what he had said.

There was an astonished silence at the other end of the line. Then the words came back to him, ominously. "This is the Bayview *Police* Department, Mr. Tabor. There are some things more important than eating."

Herb was in no mood for repentance, or apologies. "It doesn't really matter," he said. "Come along. It's just a personal preference of mine. I like my food warm, not cold."

There was the sound of a receiver crashing at the other end. "They'll probably arrest me," he told Evelyn seconds later. And what was the matter with them? he thought in bewilderment. It had been such a wonderful day — old friends seen and new friends met. Terrific messages had been preached. They had been so relaxed, were feeling so good. It wasn't fair. It was that awful telephone. It brought everyone else right into their house, invading their privacy every moment.

He said to Evelyn somewhat ruefully, "He didn't think it was funny."

"Well, honey," she said. "Don't worry. He probably won't stay long. I'll feed the kids and then wait for you." What she didn't add was that it seemed to be getting a common occurrence in their family to be eating in shifts.

"Are we going to eat by ourselves again?" asked Pam, pouting slightly.

"I'm afraid so, honey," Evelyn reassured her. "Just this once more. Then — never again, I hope."

Swiftly she got out sandwich meat, made sandwiches for the children, and heated some canned soup.

"We'll have ice cream later," said Evelyn. "When daddy can have some, too."

The children had just begun to eat their sandwiches and soup when there was a knock at the door.

Herb went to open it. "Sorry I lipped off," he apologized.

Bailey entered, nodded and said, "You know, I kind of like you. But business is business. And my business here tonight is probably going to spoil whatever is left of your day."

A solid feeling of apprehension gripped Herb. He managed to nod in acquiescence. "It already has," he said with a pained attempt at a smile.

"I'm afraid I'm going to have to take you down to headquarters with me," said Bailey.

Herb felt a wild desire to laugh, cry or shout. "Why, for heaven's sake?" he asked.

"Mr. Tabor," said Bailey, carefully, "we've had two little girls killed this past week. People in these towns are scared. Scared bad. Our department is getting a lot of pressure. Telephone calls, you know." He looked steadily at Herb and at Evelyn.

"I suppose you get them, too," said Evelyn.

"You'd better believe it, lady," said Bailey. "My boss wants to know, 'How are you coming?' The mayor of Bayview wants to know, 'How're you coming?' It gets tiresome. But," he twirled his cap, "I want to know, too."

He said politely, "If you could get your hat, or jacket, or whatever."

Herb and Evelyn exchanged incredulous glances. She moved over toward Herb, as though to protect him.

"It won't take long," said the officer. "Actually, I thought it would spare you folks something if we did it this way. Better than having a police car parked in front of your house every once in a while."

Herb nodded, and kissed Evelyn briefly. He got his light jacket and put it on. "See you later," he promised.

It was dusk outside by now, so he doubted if any of the neighbors were paying much of any attention, and the car Bailey had was an unmarked car. In a few moments they were at the police station on the north side of Bayview. Herb was taken to a room off to one side of the hallway, a room that was brightly lighted. Just like the mystery stories, Herb thought wryly. He was seated in a chair under the full glare of a center light.

There was a man at the desk, a man Herb had not seen before. He was a man with a surprisingly scholarly face for a policeman, Herb thought. He wore horn-rimmed glasses and had a pensive, thoughtful look.

"Hello, Mr. Tabor," said this officer politely. "We just want to run over with you again exactly what happened on the day Sally Ames was killed. Where you picked her up. Where you left her off. What she said to you. What you said to her."

"Where do you want me to start?" asked Herb tiredly. He suddenly realized it had been a wonderful but exhausting day. Marshalling up reserve strength from somewhere, he breathed a silent prayer and began. "I picked up Sally Ames at the corner of Blueberry Drive and the Bay Highway," he said. "She was on her way back to school. . . ."

One hour and a half later, when his stomach was growling, and his head was beginning to ache with the persistent ache it always got when he went without food for very long, the officer said, "Now, Mr. Tabor, that will be all about Sally Ames. Now we would like to hear what you did and where you went on Friday of last week."

Herb felt nauseated. His head was really aching now and his stomach hurt. Both things were from tension, he knew. And why should he feel this? It was, after all, only routine questioning. But the fact remained that he, Herbert Tabor, ordained as minister of a Baptist church, was suspect of a terrible crime or crimes. Maybe two. It was ridiculous, but there it was.

The man at the desk said, "Well, Mr. Tabor . . . ?"

It was an invitation — no, a command — to begin again. Herb began again. "It was a nice day last Friday," he said, "so I suggested to my wife that we ought to get the storm windows washed up. I got out the ladder from the church and the storm windows, and helped her wash some of the windows. Then I drove to Bayview from Anchorville about eleven in the morning to see one of our boys who is in the hospital. After that I went to a stationery store to see about stationery for the church." He went on, drawing a picture of his activities which accounted for his time up to the time he returned home from Bayview to eat his lunch at around two o'clock.

They questioned him at length. "No one went with you to Bayview?"

"No."

"But you did see a couple of persons you knew while you were in town?"

"That's right," Herb said, nodding. "I saw two men from my church in town, and talked for a moment or two with each of them."

"They weren't together, at all."

"No," replied Herb quickly. "I saw them in different places altogether. It was just that I happened to meet both of them."

"They can easily verify then that you were in Bayview at those times," said the officer. He had not introduced himself so he was nameless as far as Herb was concerned. "So far, so good," he went on. "But of course that would account for only a few minutes of your time, actually. The rest of the time you were just roaming around."

Herb frowned in annoyance. "Well, I don't know that you could really say I was 'just roaming around,' " he said. "There was the hospital call and the trip to the post office, and the trip to the stationery store and the trip to Blair's Finely Knit Shop. Not really what you'd call 'roaming.' "

"Just a term," said the man. "Well, I guess that about wraps it up, for now." It was 9:45 P.M. He looked around at Bailey, who had not uttered a word in the two and one half hours of time. "Except for one thing," said the man. "Bailey?"

"We finally found a clue today," said Bailey, looking at Herb searchingly. He opened a case he carried, took out a small folder, opened it, and handed something to Herb. "Ever see *that* before?" he asked.

Herb reached out an unwilling hand to take the small, white thing. A portent of evil assailed him. He stared at it. It was a small card, about one and one-half inches one way, two and one-half inches the other. Herb knew it well. It read:

GRACE BAPTIST CHURCH IN ANCHORVILLE
Telephone 882-3282
Rev. Herbert Tabor, Pastor
Services each Sunday at 9:45 and 11 A.M.
Evening services at 7:00 P.M.
Prayer service, Wednesday evening at 7:30 P.M.

There was a sudden dryness in Herb's mouth that clove his tongue to the roof of his mouth. He couldn't speak. He couldn't think. He could only stare at the little, white card. He knew they would not have handed it to him if it did not mean something.

"Ever see that before?" asked Bailey. There seemed to be a gleam of pity somewhere in his ice blue eyes.

"Of course," whispered Herb. "It's one of our church calling cards."

"Yours?" asked Bailey.

"Primarily mine," answered Herb.

"What do you mean, 'primarily yours'?"

"They have been passed out to various persons who have gone calling — done home visitation work for our church — so that the person visited has our church telephone." He swallowed hard. "Where . . . where did you find it?" He asked the question, knowing full well it was probably in a place that would be damning to his name.

"One of our men turned it up under a pile of lumber in the lumber yard close to the spot where Sally Ames was found."

Herb was partially prepared. He had figured something like this, but he felt as though a blow had gone all the way through him. "I didn't put it there," he said flatly.

"I hope not," said Bailey. "Like I said . . . you look like a nice young man. But who can tell anymore?" He turned and asked the man at the desk, "Do we lock him up?"

That man, the nameless ghoul, wavered before Herb's eyes. In fact, the whole room seemed to be shifting. Beyond the fact of his exhaustion, he was faint with hunger. He had been without food for about ten hours, and going without food was something he could not do. Besides that, the blow to his ego, his inner man, was devastating.

He had always prided himself on living a clean life. It had been almost an obsession with him. Ever since going into the ministry he had sidestepped evil, giving it a wide berth. He knew ministers who would, when pressed, give in to what they called "little sins" — white lies, outbursts of anger, petty gossip and other such trifles. But Herb had steadfastly set his face to do right. And now? He was so far gone emotionally that he scarcely paid any attention to what was being said. He did hear a smattering of words, "Sounds true. Can't feature it. Really can't hold him."

Bailey took him by the arm. "I'll take you home."

Herb followed meekly, even servilely. His spirit was completely crushed. When Bailey left him off in front of the parsonage, it was 10:30.

Evelyn met him at the door. "Herb!" she cried. "Where have you been all this time? It's 10:30. I finally ate a bite. The kids went to bed long ago."

Her tone jarred him further. It was so unlike her. He backed off a little and looked at her, and he knew his eyes were anything but friendly. He didn't even care.

"Where do you think I've been?" he asked. "I was down at the police station, of course." He walked past her and sat down in his favorite chair. He leaned his head back against it and closed his eyes. It was good just to sit — to sit and try to think. He sat for what must have been ten minutes. There was a complete silence in the room.

At last he heard her footsteps near him.

"Honey, please forgive me." It was a contrite whisper. "I just got so frightened. It's been such an awful week — two weeks. I just . . . just can't stand it."

He knew she was sorry, but his spirit was wounded. It was bad enough to suffer the suspicions of the police, but he had at least expected a kind word from Evelyn. He merely said, between stiff lips, "It's okay, Evelyn."

"Would you like to eat something now?"

He shook his head negatively, stubbornly rejecting the protest of his empty stomach. "I feel sick. Can't think of a thing that would taste good, right now."

"How about a cup of tea?"

She was trying hard, it was plain, to make amends, so he nodded his head in the affirmative, still keeping his eyes closed. He heard her footsteps dying away toward the kitchen, on the carpet first, then the tap tap of heels on linoleum. In a few minutes she was back with a cup of tea and a sandwich. He knew there was a sandwich, because he could smell it. It was a ham sandwich on rye, his favorite. Something inside him relaxed a little, a smile began to touch the corners of his mouth. "That's a good girl," he said. He sat up and looked at her.

Her face was pale, and there were frightened tears in her eyes. He felt a little frightened himself, because never in their eight years of married life had they ever actually been angry with each other. They had disagreed, of course, on numerous occasions, but he, the lily-white pastor, had never raised his voice to Evelyn, had never shouted, priding himself on his good, Christian temper. He took the plate from her and brushed her cheek with his lips. "Good girl," he said again. He sipped the hot tea although it burned his lips and found that, with some effort, he could manage the sandwich, even though it took some chewing.

"More?" she asked when he had finished.

"No, thanks," he said. "That's fine for now. Put a symphony on, will you, Evelyn, please? See if I can get the knots out of my head."

She went to the stereo and put on his favorite record, keeping it low so the children would not be awakened. Then she came over and sat on the ottoman next to his chair and they sat that way until the end of the record.

"Evelyn," he said when it was still. "Tonight they almost kept me there . . . at the jail."

She shot upright, stared at him incredulously, stilled into complete silence by the look on his face.

"They found one of my calling cards," he said with great difficulty, "in the lumber yard next to the lot where Sally Ames was found. It was one of mine, all right. It was a little dirty . . . had been under the lumber pile for some time."

"Herb. Have you — have you been in that lumber yard — ever, I mean?"

"Never," said Herb positively. "And I haven't been in that vacant lot, either," he added grimly.

"Well, what I meant," said Evelyn, "is that if you went there even six months ago for something, or anywhere near there, the card could have been dropped. It would have stayed."

"Through all the summer rains and winds?"

"Well, it was a thought."

"The thing is," said Herb stolidly, "that if anyone dropped my card in that lot, it simply means that, since I didn't do it, someone from our church did."

"It could have been someone from a home where our people have called," said Evelyn hopefully.

"You mean they would be carrying my calling card around with them?" asked Herb incredulously.

"Probably not," said Evelyn.

"What time is it?"

"Quarter to twelve," said Evelyn. "Bedtime."

They went to bed, but Herb lay awake until after 3:00 in the morning. There was that card. And he could not get past the fact that one of his own church members was suspicious of her own husband, had come to him with her suspicions. It could well be that he was guilty, too, if one went by the strange actions of that person. Forrest Thompson was one of the deacons and could have had a card. And should he go to the police with his story? Would they even believe him if he did? With all the many questions crowding into his mind he finally fell into a troubled sleep, dreamed of Sally Ames and her parents, dreamed he was speaking in church and Lieutenant Bailey was there to monitor his sermon. In the morning he awoke exhausted. It was light and the house was quiet, so he knew that Evelyn had gotten up and gotten Pam off to school. Reluctantly he climbed out of bed and headed for the bathroom.

It was Wednesday, and tonight was prayer meeting. How he could ever face the church people at prayer meeting was more than he could imagine. As he showered and shaved he realized that he even felt incapable of prayer. He was in such a fit of depression that he scarcely spoke to Evelyn and Donn. It was 11:00 before the spell ended, and he began to feel as though a weight had been lifted off his back.

"I think I'll go to the luncheon meeting of the Minister's Association today," he told Evelyn. "I have to get away from . . . this mess."

Evelyn nodded. "Wish I could get away from the mess," she said wistfully. The telephone had not rung all morning.

"What's the matter with the phone?" Herb asked, suddenly realizing it was silent. "Did you finally do what you said you would do?"

"I haven't touched it," said Evelyn with a little sigh. "Probably no one wants to talk to us, anymore."

"Why not?"

"Oh, I don't know."

"Ev," said Herb, staring at her. "We're acting as though we were guilty of something. We aren't. We are just the same as we were two weeks ago. I'm not going to let it get me down. I'm going to the meeting today, and enjoy myself."

He walked out the door, waving good-by as he went.

\* \* \*

Left alone, Evelyn's thoughts were preoccupied with the murders, with the police and with Herb. She sensed a moodiness in herself that was uncommon to her, a mood she was not familiar with. She felt unhappy with nearly everyone, including herself. She thought back several days to the joyous day she had experienced on Friday and wondered how it could be that such joy could disappear so soon. Twice in the past two weeks, they had experienced spiritual joy that had transcended everything; this week it was as though they had gone underground, like moles. She did her work mechanically, silent and morose.

"Mommy," Donn begged, pulling at her skirt, "mommy, I'm here." His round, anxious eyes stared up at her from his low vantage point.

"What do you want?" asked Evelyn kindly, but unenthusiastically.

"Eat?" He looked up at her hopefully. His round eyes stared at her questioningly.

"Of course, doll," she replied automatically. She fixed them a lunch, but her mind was busy with her own thoughts.

Something bothered her, haunted her, troubled her. It was an elusive something, a faint feeling of annoyance that came and went, never coming quite to the surface where she could get hold of it. It was as though within herself she asked a question that she could not answer, could not even voice the actual words. She thought back across the days of the week past. The funeral and the beauty of that day, the wonderful feeling they had had that night when the Ameses had come and had given their hearts to the Lord. It was something to do with the Ameses, she thought, something she could not quite pull out of the depths of her mind to examine, because it was buried too deeply. She recalled the day they had had the picnic and what a lovely day it had been.

She wanted to remember all of it, think back on it, savor it. She recalled how Herb had come in the door in the morning, his rather square face flushed and excited at the thought of their outing. She recalled how she had gone and put her arms around him, and how they had laughed at Donn. She recalled how she had asked about the Carmichaels and how he had told her of his visit and their deep spiritual needs and their satisfactions. And then they had driven slowly to their favorite spot on the Bay and they had talked. That was it! Like a ray of sunlight, knowledge penetrated suddenly, vividly. That was what was bothering her and wouldn't let her go.

Herb had never once mentioned to her, either at home or at the Bay when they had talked, that he had picked up Sally Ames on his way into town. He had spoken freely of the Carmichaels and had spoken enthusiastically of their plans and the church work, and everything else . . . but he had not told her about Sally Ames!

Once she had realized the thing that had eluded her, she realized she was very frightened. What if the police ever should question her? Even asked her if Herb had mentioned it to her that morning? Why hadn't he? Why had he not said, quite casually, as would be his natural way, "I gave Sally Ames a ride to school this morning." He had had such a wonderful conversation with the girl, apparently. Why hadn't he mentioned the fact? The more she thought about it, the stranger it seemed.

And there was Friday. It had started out so wonderfully, but she had been annoyed with Herb when he had come home so late for lunch. After all, she reasoned, he had left at 11:00 or shortly thereafter, and he had not gotten home until 2:00 in the afternoon. He had been detained, he had said, by the man in the stationery store, who had tried to sell him some

*113*

stationery on special, and by two of the church members whom he had met, and a couple of other things. But he had not gotten home until 2:00. How did she know where he had been, actually?

Of course, he had told her about picking up Sally Ames the night it happened, and he had volunteered the information. But he had not been like himself at all. He had seemed so tense and nervous and apprehensive. Not like Herb at all.

She ate lunch with Donn, trying to talk naturally to the child, but her mind was in a turmoil of thought, and she realized she was rambling on and on senselessly when Donn said crossly, ''Mommy, I don't like that.''

''Don't like what?'' asked Evelyn in astonishment, really looking at the child.

''What you just said,'' said Donn. He kicked his foot against the side of the chair.

''What did I say?'' asked Evelyn curiously. She suddenly realized she had spoken something out loud, something that had penetrated the small mind of her son.

''Don't truss him.''

''Truss?''

''Truss,'' repeated Donn, sublimely.

''Oh, trust,'' said Evelyn. Light broke through. She had said, she thought to herself, *I don't even trust him.* It had come out of a realization that she herself was questioning her husband.

Just then the telephone rang. Evelyn got up from her chair, and picked up the receiver. ''Hello?'' she said. She answered it cheerfully because it hadn't rung all morning. There was no answer, but she could hear heavy breathing at the other end of the line. ''Hello?'' she repeated. ''Who is it?''

There was no answer. She hung onto the receiver, feeling the skin prickling a little on her neck, and could see goose bumps rising along the fine skin of her arms. ''Hello?'' she said for the third time. Still there was no answer. After a long moment, in which the two breathings on the phone were the only sounds heard, she dropped the receiver back onto the hook. She was trembling with fright and apprehension. What a strange thing to happen! Still trembling, she went back to the dinette, and tried to get Donn to eat the rest of his pudding. The call, she realized suddenly with even greater apprehension, was actually the second of its kind. The first had come a few days before . . . last Friday? No, just Monday.

Who could have been on the phone? Someone who knew her . . . knew she was alone? Someone trying to frighten her? But why?

Donn finally finished his lunch and climbed down from his chair. His last word to her was, "Truss him."

"Thanks, Donn," Evelyn managed a tiny smile as she saw his sturdy little body start off for his favorite corner of the living room, "I will."

A few minutes later she heard their car drive in the driveway, and soon Herb came in.

"Hi, honey." He dropped a package on the table. "A small token of my affection for the one who always gets to stay home while I go out."

Obediently, and trying to feign enthusiasm, Evelyn picked up the package. Inside was a nicely wrapped box of her favorite chocolates.

"How nice," she said, smiling, "and from my favorite husband, too." For some reason she did not tell him about the phone call. He had so many worries lately, she didn't want to bother him with it. Was there another reason? She did not trust herself to even think of it. He was her own dear husband, she told herself. He was just as he had always been. Turning, she gave him a warm smile, and pushed the dark thoughts to the back of her mind. It was the now that mattered.

# 7

"WHAT DO YOU MAKE of it?" Lieutenants Bailey and Larson sat at a table in the lower section of Louie's, an Italian restaurant. Their plates were heaped with spaghetti and meatballs and Bailey was shoveling in the long strings as though it was either his last meal for a long time, or his first in a long time.

"I dunno." Larson was eating less violently. His hand moved steadily back and forth from plate to mouth, and he chewed vigorously, but he had eaten at noon; Bailey had not.

"He seems like a nice duck," observed Bailey, swallowing a wash of water. "Know what he did the day I followed him?"

"Uh-uh," Larson shook his head. He too took a swallow of water, and then he leaned back in his chair and surveyed his partner in crime detection.

"Went to the long end of the Bay. About forty miles, I guess it was. I wondered what he was going to do there, but I found out. He didn't do anything."

"Oh?"

"First he sat on a log for a while, then he got up and walked down the beach for a long ways, maybe a mile. Then he turned around all of a sudden and came back, real brisk-like.''

"Doesn't sound much like a guilty person," observed Larson sagely. "But it sounds as though he got riled up a little."

"Yeah, he was riled, all right," replied Bailey. He got hold of a piece of garlic bread and wolfed it down. "It was the morning I told them about the Kwekel kid."

"They seem like a nice couple," said Larson again.

"That doesn't mean a thing," said Bailey grimly. He took a second piece of garlic bread and attacked the spaghetti again. "Remember the Sloane case?"

"Sure, I remember it," said Larson. He reached into a pocket and took out a pipe. He knocked it on the leg of the chair, took out a pouch of tobacco, filled the pipe, and then proceeded to light it.

"Remember the girl? She was the sweetest-looking thing you ever saw."

"Yeah," Larson puffed meditatively and shifted in his chair. "Boy. Haven't you eaten for a week?"

"Hardly," said Bailey somewhat grimly. "Chief has me following him part of the time, and running to every clue that's supposedly been turned in. . . by the way. We had one again this morning."

"Oh?"

"A woman over on Temple Street called and said she saw a man apparently asleep in a parked car out on the north end of Temple on Monday last week. Was about 10:30 in the morning. She said he was there for a long time, and she thought of calling the police. Thought he was ill, or something. But she said he finally came to and drove away early in the afternoon."

"Sounds interesting," observed Larson. "What kind of car?"

"Something dark," she said. "Didn't know any makes of cars, or anything. An elderly woman, it was."

"Better check into it," said Larson. "Never can tell when a stray tip will turn out to be the real thing."

"*You* don't think Tabor did it, then?" Bailey was quick to catch the hint, and he took advantage of it readily. "Why?"

"He doesn't try to hide anything," said Larson thoughtfully, "although, there was a moment last week when we were questioning him about Sally Ames, that I thought he hesitated, and I felt he was holding something back."

"Oh?" Bailey was at last slowing down. He had pretty well demolished the plate of garlic bread, and his plate was nearly empty. "When was that?"

"You remember I asked him what Sally Ames had said to him."

Bailey nodded and gave his partner his full attention.

"Then I asked if that was all, and he hesitated, then said, 'Yes.' I have a feeling that he was holding something back."

"Well," said Bailey, rising reluctantly, and gazing once at the plate which still held a couple of slices of garlic bread, "you know how it is, Larson. You can't always remember what you said, exactly. Probably he wasn't sure."

The two men from Homicide got up and walked to the cash register, where a plump and pleasant girl took their money.

"Get enough to eat, sir?" she asked Bailey, grinning at him with familiarity.

"Sure enough, thanks, Pat," he replied, smiling back broadly. "Dunno if I can get back of the wheel again."

Turning, the two walked out the door into the late September twilight.

*     *     *

Terrified, Evelyn put the phone down cautiously, so that Herb, who was upstairs in his study, would not hear. She hoped he had not heard the telephone ring. She was shaking. The voice on the other end of the line had just said, "Mrs. Tabor, you think your husband is a nice guy, don't you? Would you like to know where he was last Friday? *I* know where he was. I saw him."

Then, there had been the sound of a receiver chucked down at the other end of the line.

"Oh." Evelyn looked at the telephone with revulsion. Then she grabbed the edge of the dinette table. She felt faint. All the fears she had pushed aside on Wednesday rushed back to confront her in all their horrifying mystery. Why had Herb been so late coming home on Friday? Why had he been so reluctant to tell her where he had been? She had asked, she remembered. He had told her he had been to the hospital; she could verify that quickly enough by calling Mrs. Evans and asking her if Herb had, indeed, been to see Tommy on Friday morning. But how could she? It would be tantamount to telling Mrs. Evans she did not trust her husband. He had said further that he had met Ben Thorpe and Ernest Rhodes at different times, so had had to stop and visit, twice. But even that should not have taken him until 2:00.

The more she thought about it, the more she was certain there was a time lapse that he had not explained to her. And this hideous caller, who was he, anyway? The other times he had been just a breath on the line, unidentifiable, eerie. Today, it had been more eerie still; a voice rough and harsh, the voice garbled, but distinguishable as that of a man — a voice that had abused her, said vile things that had made her sick. And then, the parting thing: "Mrs. Tabor, you think your husband is a nice guy, don't you? Would you like to know where he was, last Friday? *I* know where he was. I saw him."

Frantic now with fear, she dashed to the stairs, intending to call Herb. Her first reaction had been to keep him from knowing. Now, she wanted to face him with it — demand that he tell her where he had gone, why he had been so late. What he had done. She couldn't stand not knowing.

"Herb. . ." Her voice started out strongly, but ended in a kind of squeak.

There was no answer from above. She clung to the stair railing, feeling her heart pounding.

"Herb." This time it came out louder, demanding his attention. There was still no answer from above. Trembling,

119

she walked up the stairs, supporting herself sturdily with a hand that grasped the railing like the hand of a drowning man clutching a life raft. She pushed open the study door. He was not there.

The realization came to her even outside the door, when she heard no betraying sound within. She stood there foolishly, panting a little, staring at the empty room.

A moment later, sanity returned. Of course he was not there! She remembered now. An hour before he had come to the door and told her he had to make a call. He had gone to one of the nursing homes in Bayview, as they had one or two elderly members there.

She went over to his desk, saw his Bible there, and the pages of his sermon outline, lying beside it. She stared around the small room. Everything looked so normal, so everyday nice and comforting. Not frightening at all. She looked to see what he had written. It was on the Book of Ephesians, the next four verses of the first chapter. He had made notes: "Chosen in Him; holy and without blame before Him."

She opened the Bible and turned to this first chapter of Ephesians. She began to read it aloud, because it was comforting to hear the sound of her own voice:

> Blessed be the God and Father of our Lord Jesus Christ, who hath blessed us with all spiritual blessings in heavenly places in Christ: According as he hath chosen us in him before the foundation of the world, that we should be holy and without blame before him in love: Having predestinated us unto the adoption of children by Jesus Christ to himself, according to the good pleasure of his will, To the praise of the glory of his grace, wherein he hath made us accepted in the beloved.

"Accepted in the beloved," she repeated the words to herself. Then she looked out the window. It was a cloudy day, but here and there were scattered patches of blue sky showing through — a typical Michigan September day. Even as she watched the clouds, a ray of sunshine burst through the rift in them with a blinding intensity, catching her full in the face. It was like a sign.

"God," whispered Evelyn contritely, "forgive me. Make me trust *You*. I know that everything *You* do is all right. For some reason You are letting us go through the valley of the shadow of death, but I trust You, Lord." Tears began to slide down her cheeks, and she felt the terrible constriction leaving her chest. Even if her faith in her husband had been shaken, her faith in God was still all right. Turning, she retraced her steps down the stairs steadily, and with determination. She would be brave, she thought, so a chorus sprang to her lips and she sang it softly as she went downstairs:

> His Name is Wonderful; His Name is Wonderful, His Name is Wonderful, Jesus my Lord. He is the Mighty King, Master of everything. His Name is Wonderful. Jesus, my Lord.

Her spiritual thermostat resting at a comfortable high — she reached the bottom of the stairs and looked at the clock. Three-thirty. She knew that in a few minutes Pam would burst through the door, face shining and curls bouncing, to show Evelyn something precious she had made, or picked up along the way. Sometimes it was a leaf, sometimes it was a flower. Often it would be something she had made or colored that day at school.

Still fearful, but stifling her fears under a new trust, Evelyn went to the kitchen to begin preparations for dinner. Repentant toward her husband for all the evil thoughts she had had against him she decided to prepare chop suey, Herb's favorite dish. She looked in the mirror and decided her face was not too betraying. She turned on the radio, and managed to divert her scattered thoughts. She would fight. She was not going down without a struggle, she thought. No matter who it was that seemed determined to undermine her faith in herself and her husband, she would fight them with all her strength. Her own strength was small, she knew, but God's was unlimited. Vigorously, she took out the skillet.

\*　　\*　　\*

"What's for supper?" Herb came expectantly into the kitchen, sniffed the air and said in a surprised tone, "Chop suey? *Again?*"

"What do you mean, 'again'?" cried Evelyn. In a flash, all the good feeling generated by her happy preparations was gone. "You always liked it. Do you mean to tell me. . . ."

"Boy, what a short fuse," said Herb. He stood staring at her in apparent wonderment. "Are you sure you feel okay, hon? You sure are getting short-tempered, lately."

"*I'm* short-tempered!"

Herb showed his concern. He walked over, got his hand beneath her chin and lifted her face to his. "What's with you, Evelyn? All I said was 'chop suey, again.' Is that so bad?"

Evelyn could not meet his eyes. At last he dropped his hand and turned away. His shoulders drooped. It had been a rather nice call and he had managed to relax. Going to a nursing home at least took your mind off your own problems, he thought. Now, he had returned to find Evelyn in a strange and bewildering state. He couldn't understand. She was just not the same person she had been, at all.

"I'll come out for dinner when you're ready," he said through stiff lips, and walked into the living room to his chair. Donn came and climbed onto the arm. "Daddy," he intoned, stretching out both arms, and putting them around Herb's neck. "I like you, daddy."

"That's my boy," said Herb with a rush of relief and gratitude. His feelings of frustration diminished somewhat. But his ego was fast being deflated. A few more days like the last few, he thought, and he had had it. Where, he wondered, was all that wonderful Christian fortitude ministers were supposed to have? Maybe he wasn't cut out to be a minister after all, he thought. Maybe he should go into some other kind of work. *What* kind? If he couldn't handle his own wife and family, what else could he do? Exhaling deeply, he reached out and picked up the paper, cuddling Donn in one arm. Reading the paper lightly, he went from page to page. There wasn't actually much about the murders, he thought. Probably they were toning it down lest people get more upset about it. There was a brief article on an inside page, but already the current war and other affairs of the moment had crowded out the murders.

Herb read the news rather thoroughly and then looked at the "fun" page, so-called, and then Evelyn called, "It's ready."

Usually, he thought, she said, "Come on, hon, and get it." Not so tonight. His perplexity grew. Probably he should apologize for saying, "Again?" But they *had* had chop suey just a few nights before.

Out in the dinette he said, making what he thought was a masterful apology, "Sorry about the wet blanket, Ev. I always like chop suey."

"But we haven't had it lately, at all," said Evelyn. "I can't see why you said it that way."

"We had it last Tuesday night," said Herb positively. He swung Donn up to the table and put his bib under his chin.

"Herb." Evelyn turned indignant blue eyes on him. "We didn't."

"Yes, Ev, we did. But what's the difference? It's good anyhow. Forget it." Without realizing it, his tone had sharpened. He sat waiting until she sat down, until Pam had switched around in her chair and got settled to suit herself, then he offered a very brief prayer.

The much debated chop suey was good, and it tasted as good as the other had the week before. But the meal was eaten mostly in silence, and the children seemed to feel the blanket of tension.

Suddenly, the silence was broken by Evelyn's giggle, an almost hysterical titter that was totally unlike her. "I remember," she choked. "I *did* make chop suey last Tuesday. I'm sorry, honey. I must be getting old."

"It's all right," said Herb patiently, but uneasily. He thought he knew his wife like a book, but he was beginning to wonder. He had heard tales of women and how nervous they became at a certain time of life. He thought Evelyn was certainly too young to be suffering from *that*, but something sure was "eating her," as one of the older church members always said. "I shouldn't have mentioned it. You can make it every week if you like."

"No!" said Pam. "She can make chili every week. I like chili."

"I scream," said Donn. He dribbled a spoonful of sauce down his chin, and Evelyn reached over to wipe it off.

The telephone rang. Herb made a move to get up, but Evelyn pushed at his arm. "Don't!" she said sharply. Then, as the phone continued to ring, and Herb stared at her incredulously, she stammered, "I mean . . . don't bother, don't get up, honey. I'll answer it." She got up, then, and got to the phone just as it rang for the sixth or seventh time. She picked it up. "Hello?" She stood, waiting. There was no one there. Feeling a little foolish, she stood there, while Herb and the children stared at her. "There's no one there," she said, finally.

"Whom did you expect?" Herb asked the question in what he hoped was a quiet tone of voice.

In sudden realization of her peculiar behavior, she stared back at them. "No one," she said stiffly. She could feel the strain in her face, in her voice. "It's just that — you always have to get up, Herb. I thought. . . . "

Herb said, still calmly, "Is there dessert? Pie? Cake? Jello?" He said it patiently, as he would have talked to Donn or Pam.

Without replying, Evelyn went to the refrigerator and got out the dessert, a whipped cream pie, lemon. She dished it up. While she was dishing it up, the telephone began to ring again. She did not turn around.

Herb got up and answered it. "Yes, sure," he said. "Of course, anything you plan is fine with me." He talked for a minute, then came back to the table. "Sandy Jones," he said. "They want to plan a hayride for the kids next week Friday night. They make a good team for the young people's leaders." He began to eat. "Pie's wonderful," he said. "You sure make good pie, honey."

"Thank you," said Evelyn. She took a bite of the pie, but it tasted like lemon-flavored chalk to her. She fussed over Donn. "There, Donn's a good boy," she said. He beamed.

"Nice pie," he said.

"Got to go to the study for a while," Herb told her, as he got up from the table. "I'll be back around eight-thirty or nine. Church study, that is," he amplified, as he went to get his lightweight sweater. "Sure stays nice and warm for September," he remarked as he went out the door.

The conversation was so ridiculous, so inane, Evelyn could have cried with frustration. There had been a rift between them now for several days, and it was a little bit like dying. Part of the fault was her own, she admitted to herself. She had lived ever since Saturday in a curious state of unbelief and dread. Ever since the police officer had come on Saturday to tell them about the Kwekel child, she had been uneasy. Nothing had seemed right. She had no peace. Perhaps, temporarily, like this afternoon, she thought. She had managed to draw some measure of peace from her brief communication with God. And she had tried so hard. And then that silly incident of the chop suey.

Whatever was the matter with her? she asked herself. She realized, after thinking about it for a minute, that she had been so upset that afternoon she had completely forgotten that she had made chop suey only a few days before. She hoped she wasn't getting forgetful already, as some said older women got. She was only thirty-one, she reasoned, and should be too young for that, yet.

Feeling a little desperate and more than a little bewildered, she got up and began to clear the table.

Later, after she had tucked Donn away into his bed, and had read to Pam for a long half hour, it seemed to her that Herb was staying in the church study a long while. Usually when he went over to study, he studied for a prescribed length of time and then came to the house to say good-night to the children. It was now 9:00, and he had not come in. He had

125

said 8:30, but it was now a half hour later.

"Isn't daddy coming home to help put me to bed?" asked Pam. Her wide, serious eyes made a twinge of fear stab at Evelyn's heart.

"Daddy has a lot of studying to do," replied Evelyn uneasily. "He'll come over later."

"But he always kisses me good night," said Pam stubbornly.

"Won't I do?" asked Evelyn with a little laugh. "Or aren't my kisses good enough to sleep on?"

Pam got up on her lap and wound both arms around her neck, almost fiercely. "I love you, mummy," she said with frightening seriousness. "I like it when you come and kiss me good night. But daddy has to kiss me, too."

"I'll call him, and maybe he can come over, pet," said Evelyn a little shakily. She unwound Pam's arms, got up and went to the phone and dialed their line code. The phone rang twice, then Herb's voice was in her ear.

"Your daughter says you have to come and kiss her good night," said Evelyn nervously. Funny, she thought. Just the sound of his voice on the line made her nervous and trembly. She tried desperately not to let it show in her tone, but the effort made her words different, unnatural.

"What time is it?" asked Herb quietly. "I left my watch over at the house and the clock here wasn't wound yesterday."

"It's 9:00," said Evelyn.

"Okay, I'll be over," said Herb.

"Come on, Pam," said Evelyn, putting down the phone. "He's coming over, so hop into your pajamas and get ready to go to bed."

Pam promptly ran to get her p.j.'s and by the time Herb came in the door, Pam had her teeth brushed, her pajamas on, and had hopped into bed. She looked so little and frail — she was built small, like her — that Evelyn's heart suffered another twinge. What if. . . . As Herb came through the archway, she stepped aside from the bed, and went back to the living room. There she turned on the stereo softly, and got out a book. But when Herb came into the living room, he said, "How about a game of checkers?"

"Checkers? Tonight?" Her surprise was genuine.

"Why not?" His eyes were on her steadily. She tried to meet the steady gaze, but found she could not. What was the matter with her? She felt like a criminal herself, thinking the thoughts she had had today about her husband. She must not be a very good Christian herself. Where was all her faith? She had felt it this afternoon . . . when Herb wasn't there.

"Oh, all right," she said, giving in. "I'll get the board." She went to get the board and the checkers thinking, *When we get to playing, we'll both be relaxed, and I'll ask him . . . I'll say, kidding like, "You know, honey, I had the strangest call this afternoon."* She got that far in her thinking, and no further. It was as though an iron wall had come up before her. She just could not get past the thought.

She carried the board and the checkers back into the living room. With forced gaiety she put the checkers out and ran on in an inane conversation. Once she had started to pretend gaiety, she put on such a good act that she almost fooled herself. They played three games before Herb said, "It's time to quit." It was 11:30.

As the evening progressed, Herb's preoccupation deepened. His wife wasn't fooling him one bit. She had laughed, and she had smiled at him, and she had talked, but she was not herself.

"Now, Evelyn," he said, after the lights downstairs were out, and all was quiet, and they were in their room, "look at me." He came close to her, and she flinched.

It was like getting a blow to the stomach. A feeling of coldness washed over him and an almost physical pain hit him. "I don't get it." His voice was still low, almost a whisper, even though the children's room was across the hall and down a couple of doors. "What have I done that you are . . . afraid of me?"

"I don't know what you've done," cried Evelyn. "Nothing, probably. I'm just . . . nervous lately, that's all. I don't know what's wrong with me."

127

"You're lying," said Herb flatly.

Evelyn shrank away from him.

"Do you think I killed Sally Ames?" he asked, still quietly, but with a voice that she had never heard him use before.

"No, of course not," said Evelyn in a rush. "But. . . ."

"But what?" asked Herb relentlessly.

"It's so strange. You never . . . why didn't you tell me that day that you had picked up Sally in the morning?"

"So that's it." He stared at her. Now he knew what she had been hiding from him, hadn't been able to express to him. It had taken anger to drive it out of her. "So that's it," he said again, heavily. "I don't know why I didn't, Evelyn. At the time it wasn't important. So much happened after that. I went to the Carmichaels' place and just . . . well, I didn't exactly forget, but. . . ."

"And I still don't know where you were that Friday afternoon until 2:00." She had asked, and he had not told her.

A slow stubbornness was moving inside Herb. It was true he had not told her about picking up Sally Ames in the morning. Just why, he could not have told. If everything else had not happened after that, he would no doubt have told her in the evening, would have shared with her what Sally had said. But it just hadn't turned out that way. As for the unexplained lateness of Friday afternoon, he knew where he had been, and until he had gotten the sweater he wanted for her, he had no intentions of telling Evelyn. After all, he thought, he should have the right to go one place that wasn't explained.

Now he looked hard at his wife, and a feeling of anger he had never known before stirred in him. Tonight he had especially needed her closeness and her love, and it was not forthcoming. A feeling of frustration and futility came over him slowly. He felt defeated, shunned and wounded.

"Would you rather I slept on the davenport tonight?" he asked her then.

"N-no, of course not," said Evelyn feverishly. "I'm

128

not afraid of you." She laughed, and her laugh was artificial, ridiculous.

The tension between them was so tight it was like an electric current in the room. Evelyn got ready and crawled into the bed, lying as far as possible toward the edge. There were tears in her eyes as she realized that, for the first time in their married life, they had not had their devotions together. Thinking of this, she breathed a brief prayer. "Please forgive me, Lord, and help me to feel better tomorrow." She closed her eyes, she was exhausted, and in a few minutes she was fast asleep.

Herb lay on his side of the large double bed but sleep did not come. His muscles felt as though he had been lifting bricks all day, as he had on a part-time job he had had before their marriage. He wondered, as he lay there, his brain going over everything of concern to him, how he could ever get up and preach again on Sunday. Of course, that was what he had thought the Sunday before, too. And it had gone well. That was because he had let the Lord take over. That was what he must do now, he told himself fiercely as he lay there, trying not to move about, for fear he would disturb Evelyn.

But Evelyn! What could have happened to make her as she had been the past few days! Was her love for him so shallow, so material, that she could shove it aside and cast it away in a moment's time? Was he of so little account to her that she couldn't even be loyal in a situation such as they now faced? He had the sudden, sharp misgiving that things were going to get worse for him before they got better.

At last, at 4:30 in the morning, he dropped off into a fitful sleep, dreaming first that they had had news that Pam had been murdered, then that Mrs. Thompson had discovered that her husband had indeed killed Sally Ames, and then he and Evelyn went out and celebrated.

\*    \*    \*

In a hospital ward at the Bayview General Hospital, the nurse came in and checked her patient, Mrs. Vogel. The old lady had not yet recovered consciousness, and the nurse's check was methodical and brief, hurried as are nursing ministrations in most of the larger hospitals, where time and attention are at a premium.

She took the older woman's temperature, took her blood pressure and checked the fluid intake on the bottle feeding apparatus.

Mrs. Vogel's daughter was with her, and her eyes followed the nurse's every movement.

"Is she any better?" she asked, quietly enough. The nurse shook her head negatively.

"No change at all," she said.

"Do you think . . . " the daughter's word fell into the silence as a leaf falls — sudden, quiet, with only a rustle in the air. The younger woman drew her coat about her tighter, although the hospital room was warm enough.

"Do you think . . . think she's . . . going to be . . . all right?"

The nurse turned and looked at the woman kindly. "Like as not," she replied. "You'd better ask the doctor."

"I can never find him," replied the daughter in a frustrated way. "Every time I call, his office nurse says she'll have him call me, but he never does."

"Your mother is old," said the nurse softly, looking at her with compassion.

"Yes, but mother's as spry as a spring chicken," said the daughter. "And her mind is as clear as a bell. You don't know how active she is."

"Well, this will keep her down for a little while," replied the nurse, "but she has a bad fracture."

"Her arm, you mean?"

"No, I'm speaking of her skull fracture."

"Oh." The daughter looked at her anxiously, opened her lips to speak again, but the nurse was gone.

For three weeks her mother had been like this, and Anita Ozswinski shivered, facing for the first time the realization that her mother might never recover consciousness. It had seemed such a small thing, to pick up the telephone two or three times a week and chat with her mother, or run in to see her, or to take her shopping, or to the dentist, or to the doctor. What she hadn't realized was that her mother was very important to her. Now, for three weeks, instead of offering her daughter some choice bit of advice, or some droll piece of news she had gleaned from somewhere, the old lady was lying there, helpless and wasted looking.

Of course, she had her own children to look after, and her husband to care for, but . . . without her mother's love that had always reached out to her in time of need, she felt empty.

\* \* \*

Three weeks had passed since Sally Ames had died; in three days it would be three weeks since Kathy Kwekel had been murdered. And so far there was no concrete evidence; there were no clues.

Lieutenants Bailey and Larson talked about it often. They had been assigned to cover the murders full time. None of their time was to be given to anything else. They scoured the lumber yard, and they covered the distance many times between the home of the Tabors in Anchorville past Blueberry Drive, down to Sandhill Drive, and finally, to the school. There was simply nothing. Nothing, that was, that had turned up except the Rev. Herbert Tabor. The police officers were genuinely sorry about that. They had turned every corner they could think of, run down every clue given them, but all to no avail.

Bailey ate, thought, worked and slept murder. Days he sweated along with Larson on the job, and nights he dreamed. There had never before been a real murder in Anchorville. For that matter, not even a murder in Bayview, for many, many years. It had been so long ago it had been before Bailey had been on the force, and he had been on the force for fifteen years. Bailey wasn't a man who was clever at finding murderers. He was just a plain, conscientious officer who was good at keeping law and order in his territory, scrupulously honest in everything he did and he knew nothing at all about the intricacies of murder. And who did? This was a question he asked himself. Not the chief. The chief wasn't any more knowledgeable than he in that area. They might, he thought, have to call in someone from a larger city — perhaps from Lansing.

One day toward the beginning of the fourth week since the Ames girl's murder, he went down to the "morgue" of the *Bayview Bugle*. He seemed to have a feeling that, if he scanned the papers thoroughly from the day of the murder until now, he might get some clue. It was a crazy idea, he admitted to himself. A real crazy idea. But it was worth a try. So, after telling Larson where he was going so that he could be contacted in the event of an emergency, he sat himself down in the dim recesses of the "morgue," to learn what he could from the newspapers. Perhaps if he were to read the accounts of the murder again, he would get some inspiration, he thought. It had happened on a Monday . . . Monday, September 10th, because it was the Monday after Labor Day. The kids were just nicely getting back into the routine of going to school again. Ah! There was the first headline: GIRL'S BODY FOUND IN VACANT LOT: SEX DEVIATE SOUGHT IN LOCAL AREA. He read again for the umpteenth time, the story written by young Tim O'Leary. Bailey knew O'Leary. They had been at the same grim scenes and had had coffee together many a time. O'Leary was a good man, Bailey thought, as he finished the article. A little young yet, but trying hard. He methodically set himself to going down the pages minutely, one-by-one. Item by item. No item was left unread, no matter how trivial. It was thus that he found himself staring at a small item which he had never before noticed: ELDERLY WIDOW SUFFERS HOME ACCIDENT.

It was only a small notice. He would not have paid any attention at all to the notice except that the old lady lived on the Bay Highway, just south of Sandhill Drive, and that the article said that "police are investigating." Bailey sat and thought deeply. Then he read the little article again. If his

*132*

memory served him right, according to the house number given, the widow lived next to the paint store on Bay Highway, about three-quarters of a block from the school where Sally Ames had attended.

After the second reading he called his office and asked for the chief.

"Who investigated the Vogel incident?" he inquired of the chief.

"Don't remember. Vogel? Oh, the old lady. Can probably find out. Why?"

"I'm going through the newspapers to see if I can find anything at all that bears on the Ames case, and I ran across this article about the Vogel woman."

"Yeah?" The chief sounded skeptical.

"Well," offered Bailey. "The Vogel woman was taken to the hospital the same morning that Sally Ames was killed. And she lives next door to the paint store on the Bay Highway, just south of where Tabor claims he left the Ames girl out of his car. It just strikes me as a little odd that this woman, who, by the way, seems to have suffered her fall just about the time the Ames girl was murdered, should be taken to the hospital the same day. She lives on the street in question. I am just wondering if she saw anything, heard anything that would be helpful."

The chief's voice held a little more respect. "It wouldn't hurt to investigate it further," he said.

"Will you have the officer who investigated the incident call me back here at the *Bayview Bugle* 'morgue'?" asked Bailey.

"Sure thing," said the chief. There was a tiny sound of hope in his voice. "It'll take a few minutes."

"Fine," Bailey told him, and hung up. Then he went back to his papers. He immediately discarded that one, and went on to the next.

In a few minutes a girl came to tell him he had a call.

"Yeah?" he said into the phone. "Who am I talking to?"

"Van Slyke," came the voice at the other end.

Van Slyke, Bailey knew, was a new man, young, and trying hard to be a good cop.

"I'm interested in the Vogel case," said Bailey, and told the young man why.

"Don't know as I can help much," replied Van Slyke. "I was sent there to the house on a call from the daughter, because she didn't have a car available that morning, and her mother hadn't answered the phone, although she had been calling her for some time. At first she thought maybe the old lady had gone outside or to the bathroom, or something. But then, after she tried for a half hour and couldn't get her, she called headquarters and they sent me out to investigate."

"What did you find?"

"The door was locked, but I went around to the window and I could see the old lady lying on the floor with her head on the table leg. So I managed to lift one of the windows, got inside, and called the police ambulance right away. Then I called the daughter back, and she met us at the hospital emergency entrance. They admitted the old lady right away."

"Did you get a chance to talk with her?"

"Nope," replied Van Slyke. "She was unconscious. Had been for some time. The doctor thought she had a skull fracture. That's why we had to investigate it, to find out if she got the fracture in the fall, or if she was pushed or hit with something."

"What did they find?"

"Apparently the old lady had turned away from the window, knocking down a plant that was on the sill — there was some dirt on the floor near the table from the plant — caught her foot on something and fell against the table leg. That's about as much as we could figure out."

"Thanks a lot," said Bailey. And he meant it. Because here was help at last. There was one sentence in the officer's report that interested him mightily. It was that the old lady had been at the window before she fell.

He almost ran back to the table, got his cap, and hurried out the door. He was on his way to see the house where Mrs.

Vogel lived. After that he would go to the hospital.

In front of the house on the Bay Highway Bailey got out of the cruiser, went up to the door, and slipped the key into the lock. It turned easily, and he went in, looking about him as he went. The house had a slightly musty smell, as old houses do after being shut up tightly for several days, and, in this particular case, weeks.

But Bailey was interested in only one thing: the window with the plants. He quickly saw the table where Mrs. Vogel had fallen. From there he lifted his eyes and saw the window . . . the window that looked out on Bay Highway, and the sidewalk in front of the paint store. Bailey walked up to the window, picked up the plant, and looked. Quite a view of the street, he thought. Mrs. Vogel could well have seen the girl — could have seen the murderer.

Sudden excitement shot him into action. He put the plant down carefully. It had been watered, he noticed. Probably the daughter had come and taken care of things. The house looked neat and clean. He must go to the hospital and see Mrs. Vogel. For the first time in three weeks, hope flared within him. Moving quickly, he slid away from the window, hurried to the door, went out, locked it behind him and drove to the Bayview Hospital.

# 8

O H! HERB!'' said Evelyn as she put down the phone and turned to him. ''Mrs. Evans' brother just called. Tommy has taken a turn for the worse. He's developed pneumonia, or something, and is quite bad. They want you at the hospital.''

''On my way,'' said Herb, grabbing his hat and jacket from the hall closet. ''I'll call you when I find out what's what.'' He paused briefly to give her cheek a brush with his lips. They had made up after a fashion the day before, and both were trying desperately to be themselves.

Herb drove the distance to the hospital in near record time. His last visit with Tommy had been a little more fruitful. It seemed that he had, at least, convinced the boy that *he* cared. If he could only convince him that God cared. . . .

The hospital was getting to be a familiar place and he felt he could almost find his way around the second floor pediatrics section blindfolded. He had made it a practice that, every time he came to see Tommy Evans he also dropped in on some of the other children in the wards. The children in the private and semi-private rooms were nearly always well-visited. But some of the children in the wards Herb had learned were neglected children — children who had been brought in to the hospital by "conveyors" — persons who made a living transporting children to hospitals and clinics. Sometimes, Herb had learned, the conveyor would be the only visitor a child would have. Some of the children were from the upper part of the state, and their parents could not visit often. Now, not bothering to look into the wards, Herb went rapidly upstairs to the second floor and turned left to Room 255.

One look told him the matter was serious. There was a sign on the door: NO VISITORS. Pastors were exempt from the restriction, of course. Herb went in. Mrs. Evans was sitting at the foot of the bed and there were tear stains on her cheeks. Mr. Evans sat next to the bed at the left, holding Tommy's hand. The boy's eyes were closed. He looked flushed and hot and he tossed every minute or so, mumbling in his sleep.

"Oh, pastor!" whispered Mrs. Evans. "Pastor . . . he . . . he . . . the doctor said he's afraid he's not going to make it!"

"Really?" Herb was shocked. The boy seemed much improved when he had seen him two days before and he had thought then that he was out of danger. "What's wrong?"

"They aren't sure. They thought first he had pneumonia. Now they think he has somehow got some other severe infection. And you know Tommy is so allergic to everything. They don't dare give him the antibiotics they ordinarily would give."

At that moment the doctor and a nurse came in. The nurse stuck a thermometer in the boy's mouth. His eyelids fluttered, but he did not open his eyes. Mrs. Evans leaned forward. "What do you think, Dr. Barnes? Is Tommy any better?"

The doctor looked directly at Tommy's face, put his hand on the boy's forehead, ran a practiced hand over his body. The hand halted on Tommy's stomach. "What do we have here? Ah! What I was afraid of." Dr. Barnes turned to the parents and his eyes were soft with pity. "You have a very sick boy here," he told them. "Very sick. He has peritonitis. This is a complication of his surgery of the other week. Tommy is not strong at best. We will do our best, that's all I can promise.''

He pressed the buzzer for another nurse and presently an R.N. flashed in, crisp white skirts rustling. ''There is a possibility we can do surgery,'' Dr. Barnes went on. ''He would have a 50-50 chance. Without it, his hopes are nil.''

''Surgery? Again?'' whispered Mrs. Evans. Her eyes went wide with new alarm. Mr. Evans went close to her and put his arm around her.

''Now, Alice, you know the doc is doing everything he can.'' There were tears in his eyes, however, and Herb knew they both realized the extreme gravity of the situation.

Herb motioned them to follow him out into the hall, and he led them down a few doors to a small waiting room that was empty. The three of them sat.

A nurse came and said, ''You will have to sign, Mr. Evans — the permission to operate.''

The Evanses looked at each other, a long, searching look. ''If it has to be,'' said Mrs. Evans in a barely audible voice. ''If it's the only chance.'' Then she broke down, sobbing. ''I can't stand it,'' she said. ''I can't. How can God be so cruel? Our boy . . . our only boy. And Mr. Tabor, it wouldn't be quite so bad . . . quite so bad, if I knew that Tommy believed. But he doesn't, really. You know that.''

Herb nodded miserably. She was voicing his own troubled thoughts. The boy had been surprisingly hard and unreachable in all the visits they had had, at least until two days before.

Evans disappeared down the hallway on his hated mission.

Herb thought desperately that he should be able to say, in a deep, comforting voice, ''Now, we'll just pray for Tommy, Mrs. Evans, and it will be all right.'' But it was as though his lips were sealed. He couldn't think of any of the right things to say. Something seemed to hold him back. He sat there silent, wondering frantically if it was because of his own harrowing experiences of the past three weeks, his own emotional involvement. Was it due to his own lack of faith? Why, three weeks ago he had touched the sky — he had touched God.

Presently Evans came back. Herb thought he had to say something to comfort the two of them and he fought a strange power that had him in a strangle hold. He opened his lips and said, "We can ask God that His will be done." They both nodded. They were good Christian people, Herb knew, so the matter of real concern was how they took the news if it should be bad. He prayed with them, asking the Lord to spare the boy if it was His will; asking the Lord to give the parents strength to accept whatever the outcome might be.

Forty-five minutes had passed when the doctor came in. He had tears in his eyes. He went up to Mr. Evans and took his hand. "It is never easy to tell anyone this," he began haltingly. Then, very simply. "I'm sorry. We did our best."

It seemed a long five or ten seconds passed while the three in the waiting room accepted what he said. Then Mrs. Evans seemed to gather a great strength from somewhere outside herself. "It is God's will," she said, and laid her face against her husband's chest.

Herb felt strain in his face. He wanted to cry, felt he could, but no tears fell. A kind of numbing paralysis had laid hold of him, and it seemed he could not express himself as he should. He swallowed with some difficulty and offered to stay with them.

"If you could stay just a little while," Mrs. Evans said. "Then some of our relatives will probably come. As soon as we decide where to have them take Tommy."

"I'll call my wife, and let her know that I'm staying," said Herb. He walked down the hall to the pay telephone and made the call, telling Evelyn the situation. "Tell you all about it when I get home," he said.

He spent another half hour with the Evanses until Tommy's body had been removed to a funeral home in Bayview. He left them then after assuring them both that he would be praying for them, and would be looking in on them in the evening. Even though it was a sad occasion it did thrust him back into his accustomed role of pastor-counselor. His heart was heavy though with the realization that he had not brought Tommy Evans to the Great Shepherd. A failure, it seemed, yet, God was just, he knew, and Tommy was in God's hands.

As he reached the first-floor corridor he saw a familiar blue-clad figure coming toward him.

"We meet again," he said, stopping a moment.

"Yes," returned Bailey, smiling. "I see you are at your business, and I am following through on mine."

Herb lifted his eyebrows quizzically. "You track them to the hospitals too, eh?" he said, trying to be friendly.

Bailey nodded, his eyes sharp and yet kindly. He seemed to hesitate, and Herb felt a stab of intuition. He felt that Bailey wanted to say something so he made another verbal offering. "Not another injured child!"

"Not at all. This patient is quite elderly," said Bailey. "She has a skull fracture. She's been here for three weeks and hasn't come to yet."

"Who is she?" asked Herb. All his pastor's sympathy was aroused now.

"Name's Vogel," said Bailey, jerking his thumb back over his shoulder. "She fell in her home and struck her head on a table leg. Bad skull facture, doctor says."

"Oh," said Herb. "That's too bad. Does she have relatives?"

"A daughter who comes every day and sits with her," said Bailey.

"So many people in hospitals don't have anyone," said Herb. "It's bad enough for adults, but the children get me . . . there are a lot of kids here from broken homes, orphans, and the like that nobody ever comes to see. I've been trying to drop by and say 'hello' to some of them when I come to visit our boy." He paused, remembering. "But I won't be coming any more to see him," he said.

"Oh?"

"He died today. He had peritonitis. They operated, and he didn't make it. That means another funeral."

"You have it?"

"Yes," said Herb. Involuntarily, a slight shudder went over him.

"That's two kids in three weeks," said Bailey, clicking his tongue against his teeth. "Hard on you, I imagine."

"Yes," said Herb again. Somehow he felt older than he had when he had started down the stairs.

"Why don't you stop by and see the old lady?" asked Bailey suddenly. "The daughter might appreciate it."

"Well," said Herb slowly, "they probably already have a minister who comes. I might not be welcome."

"I don't think so," said Bailey.

"What room?" asked Herb, making a sudden decision.

"One-fifteen," said Bailey. "Just through the swinging doors down there." He pointed back the way he had come.

"I'll drop in and see her tomorrow morning," promised Herb.

Bailey started to walk away, hesitated, and came walking back. "You might . . . say a little prayer for her, while you're there," he said. "I kind of need her for a case I'm working on."

He walked off without further words.

Herb stood looking after the officer, a puzzled frown on his face. He would pray for Mrs. Vogel, all right. But that was a strange way to go about it . . . to pray for someone to get well because they were needed for a "case." Well, he mused as he walked slowly down the hallway toward the door, he had seen many strange things in the past few weeks, and should be getting used to them.

\*　　\*　　\*

The murderer was a lonely man. In a way, he thought, he had always been lonely. But now a great distance seemed spread between himself and the rest of the world he knew. He walked a dangerous and a lonesome road. As far as his wife was concerned, she seemed not to notice that he was anything different from what he had been. He presumed it was because she was probably too engrossed in her own pursuits, pursuits that seemed to be of very great importance to her. If he had become a little more distant, a little moodier, no one seemed to know, or care.

The main enjoyment he got now was from his books. He kept them handy and read avidly when he got the chance. There was one that gave him more thrills than the others. It was a book on black magic. He had picked it up one day in a drugstore where he had gone to get some aspirin. It was a store he did not usually frequent, and he had spotted the several books and magazines with interest. He had always had a natural bent toward the occult, anyhow. Christians weren't supposed to be interested in such things, he knew, but the fact remained that he was. But, then, he thought, maybe he wasn't a real Christian.

At any rate, from the day he had picked up the book with its black cover and red title, *Black Magic*, he had been enchanted. Of course he had it hidden where no one was likely to find it . . . in the garage, underneath a pile of oiled rags.

He had wondered at first, if there was anything to it . . . the bit about Satanic powers being nearby and available if one would only get in contact with them. Of course, the Bible talked about ''demonic powers'' and the like. The thought of such things had always fascinated him. Now, when he heard someone in the church talking about the devil and his workers, he would smile secretly. A lot *they* knew about it! He could tell them, plenty, he thought. But that would ruin everything. At times he would be somewhat fearful of the final outcome, and he would break out in a cold sweat. But he was being led on inexorably now, and it was vastly exciting. He had a feeling of power and personal awareness he had never felt before, even when he ''got saved'' at church, when he was a boy. It had been a good game all these years, he thought often now. But a game that had brought him few rewards.

It hadn't been so bad, he recalled, until that Dilson had come to church with his ''deeper life'' talk. At first he had wanted this; but it seemed the more he prayed and asked God for blessing, the farther away from Him he felt. What he really wanted to do was to heal and to speak in tongues, like the Bible told about. That would be really living, he thought. It would be like New Testament times today. He could travel around and pray and heal, like some men he had heard of.

Well, it hadn't worked that way at all. The way it had worked was that he had begun to doubt that he had any contact with God at all. Then he began to doubt if he was truly a believer at all. The more the preacher preached, the more he felt annoyed — with himself, with God, with the preacher. And after the young one had come — for a year now — he had become almost immune to anything that was said. He had had the books for a year — he had bought them just before Tabor had come. Now, when he would get to the service his mind seemed to wander. And lately, there had been all the strange fantasies that had finally culminated in reality. It was a reality he did not exactly enjoy, but a reality he could not escape, even if he had wanted to.

There had been excitement and fever in the conquests of his victims, but that had passed. Now he lived each day with the cold knowledge that he was a wanted man. There was little chance they would catch him at all, he thought. They had a beam on the pastor, and he had helped *that* along. But it was the preacher's wife he really hated.

From the first day he had set eyes on her he had despised her oval, open face, her sparkling eyes and quick smile. She was too much of a "goody girl," as he mentally termed it. She was just too nice. Her trouble was, he thought viciously, that she really believed what she said she believed. He had never heard her raise her voice, never seen her frown at anyone. He had never known her to say anything harsh about anyone in the whole year. It was too much. Contrasted with his own wife, she drove him mad.

Lately, though, he had been heartened by a certain wistfulness in her eyes, a certain firming of the muscles around her mouth, a certain turning down of the corners of the mouth that had always smiled. He had had an inspiration when it came to the telephone calls, he thought. They had been directed by his new boss, Satan.

Now he stepped out of the telephone booth and wiped his handkerchief across a streaming forehead. Hadn't even been worth the effort this time, he fumed. No answer. Well, he could try again. There was always another time . . . another tomorrow. A cynical smile creased his face momentarily and was gone. He walked slowly down the street and got into his car. Some of the anticipation had gone out of the evening.

\*     \*     \*

Monday, October 1st. The two officers drove slowly around the street as they had done many times before. There was a frown on the usually genial face of Larson.

"The old lady came to, you said?" he asked in an awed tone. "She really did?"

"She did," said Bailey with some satisfaction. "I thought she would."

"How come? The doc said she probably wouldn't regain consciousness at all."

Bailey looked earnestly at his companion. "She had outside help," he said mysteriously.

Larson's forehead creased even more. "What d'ya mean?" he asked. He wasn't a stupid man by any means, but he did not possess a great imagination.

"It's really quite funny, in a way," replied Bailey. "You see, I met the preacher in the hospital one day after I had gone to see the widow, and I told him he might drop in to see this patient. Well, he did, the next day. I told him also that he might pray for her, as I needed her for a case I was working on." He turned to survey his companion and saw a delighted smile on Larson's face.

"Well," he continued, steering the Chevrolet skillfully around another corner. "She regained consciousness yesterday. She didn't know her daughter then, but today she recognized her. The daughter is beside herself with joy."

"Did you get to question her at all?"

"Nope," said Bailey. "She can't remember anything yet. But when she does, it's going to help us in this case I know."

"You think she saw the murderer?"

"Yup."

They were by this time coming along the street next to the vacant lot where Sally Ames had been found. Bailey turned in and drew up to the site once more where the girl's body had been found. There were neat, flat pegs marking the exact spot. The grass around the spot had been trampled by many feet coming and going.

"There has to be something," said Bailey grimly. "There has to be." He turned off the motor and got out.

"Funny we've never been able to find a weapon," said Larson. He climbed out of the car and stood beside Bailey.

"Can't figure it," replied Bailey. "We've had men looking all over the place. But there had to be something to make all those bruises. And when we find it, it'll help our case."

"It wouldn't be anything sharp," said Larson. "There weren't any cuts."

"Right." They both stood looking down at the pegged space. In retrospect they saw a lifeless body lying grotesquely in the weeds.

"Maybe if just the two of us measured off a space up and down the lot with a line of string and then went up it together, then marked out another line and went over that until we covered every part of this lot, inch by inch, we could find something. If necessary," Larson added, looking at the stack of lumber nearby, "we'll make 'em take that stack of lumber down piece by piece so we can look under it."

Bailey agreed. Larson had brought along a ball of twine and now he got it out of the car. He first tied one end of the twine around a stick he picked up from the ground. Then he carried it over to the edge of the lot, paced off four steps, and shoved the stick into the ground. It had rained the night before and the stick went in easily. Then Bailey paced off four steps at the other end of the lot, and straightening the string to a taut line he put the stick at the other end of the twine into the ground. Then, beginning at the north of the lot, the two of them walked shoulder to shoulder up the line, spreading the grass with their feet and looking at every inch of ground. In this way they covered the first space. Then they placed a stone at one end of the lot near the stake and moved the line over another four paces. About halfway down the third section they came to a large clump of burdocks.

"Push them over," said Larson. He put out a hand and pushed, hard. The burdocks were so strong it took some effort to bend them over. Bailey took out a pocket knife and sawed away at a couple of stalks until they broke over. He growled as he brought his hand back. His sleeve was adorned with a large clump of burdock burrs. He threw them off into the section already covered. Then his eyes caught sight of something under the burdock. A loud exclamation of jubilance escaped him as he reached down. "Here it is! I knew it had to be here!" He picked up the object and turned it over in his hand. It was a flashlight. "I should be wearing gloves," he said. Then his eyes widened. He swore under his breath and his face puckered as though he were going to cry.

"Wouldn't you know," said Larson, peering at it. "Too bad. Too bad."

Bailey nodded. For the moment he could not speak. Then a thinness came across his mouth and a sardonical smile fled briefly across his face. "I might have known," he said bitterly.

In his meaty hand he held the flashlight, dented on one end, scratched. The identification marker on it showed faintly the initials: "H.T."

\* \* \*

"I can't believe it," said Herb. "It can't be."

"Is it your flashlight?" the question came at him so brutally that it was like a body blow.

He flinched and looked again. "Yes, it is. I had that plate put on it because someone is always borrowing it and I

146

thought that would be a good way to keep it from turning up missing.''

''Had you missed it, then?''

''No . . . not that I recall. If I did, I just borrowed the one in the house.''

Herb was sweating now. A few days of peace had somehow put to rest all his fears. He had been eating better; he and Evelyn had made up and everything was just about back to normal in their household — as normal as it could be when a break in a relationship has been made and repaired. And the repair was only rough — they both knew it.

''Tabor, I'll have to arrest you.''

''No!'' The word burst from his lips, which instantly became dry and unmanageable.

''Sorry, but this is it, I'm afraid,'' said Larson and Bailey almost together.

''The party is over,'' said Larson.

Evelyn came into the living room. ''Wha . . . hat is it?''

''They're arresting me,'' said Herb. Their eyes met, his unbelieving and bitter, hers fearful and withdrawn. At the look in her eyes, Herb's shoulders sagged. He felt as though he had been run over by a truck. Abjectly, he let the officer take him by the arm and lead him out the door.

\*     \*     \*

Evelyn stood in the center of the room. Her hands were pressed to her temples and tears of fright coursed down her cheeks. Strangely enough her fright was not for her husband. It was for herself. The first thoughts that fled through her mind were, *What will the church people think? Am I married to a murderer? How can I ever face people again? How can Pam go to school when people will know her father is in jail?*

So great was her agitation that she found she was whispering to herself, wildly, feverishly. ''No. No. It can't be. No one will speak to me. I can't face it.''

\*     \*     \*

By 10:00 that night news broadcasts had proclaimed the news to an excited public. "Killer of little girls thought apprehended. Minister arrested on circumstantial evidence."

The telephone in the parsonage rang almost constantly. One church member after another called. Some of the calls were comforting; others were subtle, little barbed innuendos permeating the conversations. Somehow through it all Evelyn managed to maintain a false composure, somehow making answers automatically, her favorite rejoinder being, "I don't know. I don't know."

A final call caused her to break. The caller was Anne Rhodes and she made a remark that set Evelyn's teeth on edge.

"After all," she said in a purring voice, "none of us really knows another, no matter how long we live with them."

"I know my husband!" shouted Evelyn before she could think, or choose her words, "And I'd rather live with him than with anybody else on earth!"

There was a sudden, shocked silence on the other end of the line, then the click of a receiver being hung up. Evelyn didn't care. She suddenly had returned to sanity. The words she had just shouted into the telephone were true. She did know her husband; she believed in him, and she would rather live with him than with anyone else on earth. The renewed knowledge brought tears of joy falling rapidly down her cheeks, the relief was so sudden and so great. She sat down on the davenport in the living room and wept brokenheartedly. Not for herself, now. For her stricken husband, who was even now separated from her, maybe forever.

There was a knock at the door. Evelyn did not immediately respond. She was just thankful that the children were in bed where she had sent them just after the officers had taken Herb away. Now she didn't want to see anyone. She just wanted to go to bed, sleep it off . . . if she could. She knew she must. For the sake of the children. For Herb's sake.

The knock was repeated. Evelyn got up numbly, sweeping back a lock of hair that had escaped her hairband, and wiping one hand swiftly across her eyes. She got to the door and opened it.

The woman outside almost literally fell into her arms. It was Anne Rhodes.

"Oh, Mrs. Tabor, forgive me, forgive me," said the woman breathlessly. She was grasping Evelyn tightly by both arms. She was weeping. "I'm so sorry I said what I did. It was perfectly awful of me. The Lord convicted me the minute I put the phone down. Please . . . please. Let me stay here tonight with you. I'll sleep on the davenport and answer the phone if it rings. Anything."

"That's all right," said Evelyn. She put her head down on the older woman's shoulder and let the tears flow freely. "Forgive me, too. I shouldn't have shouted like that. I — haven't been myself lately, at all. But you brought me to my senses. Until you called I *had* been doubting Herb. I've been wondering if I really did know him. I've been getting phone calls. . . ." She stopped suddenly, aware that she was telling Anne Rhodes something she had not even told her husband, much less the police. She actually had been withholding evidence.

"Phone calls?" Anne Rhodes' eyebrows lifted swiftly. "What kind of calls?"

Should she tell? Evelyn hesitated. "I really shouldn't talk about it, I guess," she said. "But it really was those phone calls that set me off."

"How many phone calls? What kind? Who from?"

Evelyn thought back. "There were three phone calls when nothing happened," she said. "Only I would go to the phone, and there would be somebody there, just breathing. Not saying anything. Just breathing." She shivered, remembering. "And there was one, a horrible one — just a week or two ago — that was what started most of the trouble. . . ." She stopped again, uncertain if she should tell any more. Not until she had told the police.

"Started what trouble?" Anne Rhodes prodded gently. It didn't seem possible that she could be the same person

149

who, just an hour before, had insinuated things over the telephone.

"Trouble," said Evelyn, "in our house. Between Herb and me. It was my fault." She stopped, suddenly, exhausted. "I'm going to bed and lie down," she said. "You will stay? Then I can rest in peace." She left Anne sitting on the davenport and went up to their bedroom, but she could not bear the thought of that double bed alone. So she went down the hallway to the "spare bedroom," and taking off her clothes drearily, lay down and was soon mercifully asleep.

*     *     *

In his cell at the jail, Herb had lost all feeling of reality. He had tried to pray, once when the officers had brought him in. But try as he might, words would not come. Gone was the assurance he had had of God's presence. Gone were all the lofty thoughts he had mouthed in earlier days. Like a funeral pall a dark cloud overshadowed him. One of the bitterest things was Bailey's almost brutal treatment. He had shoved him into the cell like a common criminal. Which, he thought glumly, they seemed to think he was. He had begun to have grave doubts about himself.

There was Evelyn, for instance. Why should she suddenly doubt him — turn her back on him? What had he done that she should treat him like that? All over one ridiculous omission of statement from him? Was there no belief in others anymore? Hadn't he been a good husband to her? He remembered the veiled look in her eyes as the officers had led him out the door. For Herb, it was the end of his endurance.

Strangely enough, ever since the officers had showed him the flashlight with his initials on it, Herb had experienced self-doubt. He had begun to wonder, a trifle madly, if perhaps he might be guilty. He thought he could remember every move he had made on that fatal Monday. But perhaps there was a blank — a gap he could not fill. He had studied enough psychology in his schooling so he knew of persons with split personalities, persons who, though seemingly outwardly "good persons," actually became other personalities at times and performed things they would not have dreamed of doing in their right minds. Was he one of those? Was he a schizophrenic? Was he really an assaulter of little girls, hiding behind a facade of clerical interest? Herb thought and thought, tormented by strange forces that beat his conscious thinking into a maze of doubt and apprehension.

Lying on the hard cot in the cell he finally fell asleep from sheer exhaustion.

*　　*　　*

"Men, I tell you this thing cannot be!" It was Carmichael, speaking in strong language to the assembled deacons of the church. There they sat, staring back at him like so many owls on their perches, Rhodes at the far left, Thompson next, O'Neil in the middle, and Johnson at the far right. No one seemed disposed to say much to anyone else, and each man seemed to be trying to avoid the eyes of the others.

"It's a disgrace to the church," said O'Neil flatly. He stared at the floor, a frown between his eyes. "People at work asked me about it this morning. I didn't know where to go."

"Disgrace, my foot," snapped Carmichael swiftly. He looked at the men in front of him. "There's no disgrace involved in anything, if you are innocent."

There was considerable foot-shifting and then an uncomfortable silence.

"He's too valuable a person to leave in jail, like this. A few thousand dollars bond. That's all we need. The church could easily post this."

"How do we know he's not guilty?" Finally, one of the men had the courage to speak up. It was Forrest Thompson. He didn't look well; his eyes were rather strange, thought Carmichael, and there was a mask-like look to his face.

"I know, because I know what kind of man he is," retorted Carmichael. "Further, I know where he was at 9:00 in the morning the day of the murder. He was at our house, because we asked him to come."

"Could have done it, then come to your house."

Carmichael denied this hotly. "Not if you had been there, you couldn't say that," he insisted. "He was his natural self. He talked to us, helped us. He said he and his wife were going to go on a picnic later in the morning."

"Did he tell you he picked up Sally Ames on the way to school?" This time it was Carl Johnson who posed the question.

"No," answered Carmichael. "Why should he? We weren't interested in Sally Ames. Until she was dead, there just wasn't that much interest in her. She was just another member."

"Maybe that's what's wrong with our church," suggested Ernest Rhodes from his position at the left. "Each of us should be terribly important to the other, all the time."

Two heads nodded in agreement. Thompson's head nodded, then dipped strangely almost, Carmichael thought in surprise, as though he had no control over it.

"I didn't know there was anything wrong with the church, until this happened," said O'Neil smoothly. "I was pretty satisfied with it, myself."

"I wonder if the Lord is satisfied with it," said Rhodes then. He straightened up suddenly and holding himself somewhat rigidly, his glance swept over the others. "Here we are, doubting our pastor. When we called him, we said, 'This is God's man for us.' Now we are saying maybe he is a killer. It doesn't make too much sense, when you think of it."

"Those are my thoughts exactly," said Carmichael. "I know I can't do it myself, because I'm not a deacon, but it seems to me that the church should get him out of jail, because the longer he's in there, the worse it's going to look."

"I don't think the church would go along with that," said O'Neil. "That is a lot of money. Besides, I don't even know if we have that much."

"Then," said Carmichael, "my wife and I will put up the money ourselves. And I won't keep you any longer, gentlemen.'' He picked up the light jacket he had worn there and slipped into his pocket the New Testament he always carried. Nodding slightly to the other men, he left the room.

*   *   *

There was a rattle at the door of his cell, and Herb came to with a start. The man who entered was a man whose face he could remember . . . where had he seen him and when? Lately?

"Morning, Tabor," said the older man, sticking out a strong hand. "Dilson. Remember me?"

"Oh, yes," replied Herb. His memory surprisingly sprang back out of its limbo to the meeting at Willow City a week or so before. "How are you?"

"Just great. And how are *you?*" The man's words were pointed and meaningful. A uniformed figure stood just outside the cell, Herb noticed and he lowered his voice.

"Not so good," he said. He shied away from the older man's gaze, and looked uneasily around the bare cell.

"God sometimes lets us pass through deep waters for a purpose," said Dilson. "Isn't that what you've been telling other people lately?"

Herb nodded. He thought he should feel ashamed, but he didn't. He had only a feeling of numbness.

"Then why is it so different for you?" The older man prodded gently, but strongly, into his wounds and they opened up and bled.

Herb told him everything — how his confidence had been shattered by Evelyn's increasingly strange behavior and the fact that the police had found two items of evidence against him in the vacant lot.

"Doesn't sound like much," Dilson said without much sympathy.

"It wasn't actually," said Herb. "But I've got to thinking now, 'What if I *did* do it?' There are lots of people like that — people who look good on the outside, but who are rotten on the inside. Maybe I'm one of those."

153

For half an hour longer the older pastor talked with Herb and prayed with him, then left with the word that he would be back the next day. That made the visit really meaningful to Herb because Dilson's church was about sixty miles away. None of the other area association pastors had been to see him, Herb reflected. Of course, it was only the second day . . . but Dilson had come.

When Dilson left Herb had a feeling that was somewhat better, but there was still an ache in his heart that was actual and physical. As far as his self-doubts, those had diminished mainly, but he still felt unclean and drained.

\* \* \*

"Mr. — Lieutenant Bailey," said Evelyn breathlessly, "I've got to talk with you. Got to tell you something I've been holding back."

"Yes?" The Lieutenant's face was red, stolid, with no expression whatever that she could see.

"It's the telephone calls," said Evelyn. "The telephone calls were what hurt us — what made me ornery."

"Start at the beginning," ordered Bailey brusquely.

"The first time," said Evelyn, "Herb was gone somewhere, and the telephone rang. I answered it, but there was no answer. Just someone breathing at the other end."

"You could hear a person breathing?"

"Yes." Evelyn shivered, remembering. "I wouldn't have thought too much about it except that, with the two murders, everything was different somehow."

"When was the next one?"

"It was probably close to a week later. It was the same thing. I don't know how to say it, except that it was eerie, weird. I could feel someone was there, and hear him breathing."

"What did you do?" Bailey turned a searching gaze on her, measuring her.

"I hung up."

154

"Did you slam the phone down, or make any remark?"

"I don't think so," said Evelyn. "Why?"

"The main pleasure a person gets out of such calls is the irritation they cause. They don't hurt anyone, of course, they are what we call 'nuisance calls'."

"Oh, but the last one was different!" said Evelyn with a rush. "The last time, the person said all kinds of obscene things to me, then said, 'I can tell you where your husband was on Friday. I saw him.'"

"Really?" At last she had struck a spark, she thought. Bailey really looked at her — not through her, but at her — and his eyes had lighted up. "That's very interesting. Was your husband home at the time of this last call?"

"No," said Evelyn. "I thought he was. I've been pretty upset lately. I ran to the stairs and called him, I was going to ask him if what the caller said was true."

"Ah." Bailey sat back in his chair and surveyed her with compassion. "So. You have been doubting your husband."

A red tide swept up Evelyn's face and throat, then subsided, leaving her extremely pale. "Yes, I have," she said. "This is what has been wrong about it."

"Why did you doubt him?"

Evelyn stared back at the officer. She was trapped and she knew it. She hadn't intended to tell him everything, but here she was, because Anne Rhodes had told her she should come, had said it might be very important to Herb, if the police knew about the phone calls.

"Come, Mrs. Tabor. There must have been a reason. Why?"

"Because," said Evelyn breathlessly, as fear consumed her again. "Because the day Sally Ames was murdered, I found out — he told me — that he had picked her up in the morning, and taken her to school. But all the time we were together Monday, he never told me. I couldn't understand why. It would just seem such a natural thing to do. We always tell each other everything."

"He could have forgotten," said Bailey. His gaze lowered to the desk and he shuffled some papers around on it.

"But he *hadn't* forgotten it . . . he told me that night . . . at supper. He said he was scared, because he thought he must have been the last person except for the murderer, to see her alive."

"There may have been one more," Bailey said the words, then pressed his lips together. "Shouldn't have said that. Don't want to give you any false hopes. Not much chance anyway. Forget that I said it."

"You mean . . . you've found a witness?" Hope flared and leaped in Evelyn as she whispered the words.

"Possibly. But don't get your hopes up."

Bailey questioned Evelyn further, for some twenty minutes. Then he arose. "I won't keep you any longer, Mrs. Tabor. I can't tell you how much I appreciate your having come down here. I know it wasn't easy for you."

"Thank you," said Evelyn. She stood up and stared at him hard. "Now, I'd like to see my husband," she said.

Staring at Herb across the long table, with the guard down the hall trying to look unconcerned and unlistening, Evelyn broke down again. It seemed to her that was all she had done for two days was cry. But she knew it was good for her. Tears were good for her, she told herself as she choked them back. "I can get down on my knees if it will make you feel better," she said in a loud whisper.

"Why should you want to get down on your knees?"

"I've been a fool," said Evelyn. "I doubted you. And I love you, Herb, I really do. I *really* do!"

She looked across the table at her love and saw that a tightness that had been in his face every day for some time was relaxing. "Say that again," he commanded her.

"I really do," repeated Evelyn obediently.

"Really what?"

"Love you, you big ape!" said Evelyn, losing patience.

"Now you sound more like yourself," said Herb. A smile began at the corners of his mouth and spread across his face. "You were too polite before."

"I'm always polite to you," said Evelyn, her chin beginning to quiver again. "Except when . . . when . . . I'm under a terrible strain, like the last few weeks. You might allow me a little temper, Herb. *You* have some."

"Of course I'll allow you a little temper, sweetheart," said Herb, looking at her with intense longing in his eyes. "I love you anyway, temper or no temper."

"We've always tried to be too nice to each other," said Evelyn. "It isn't natural. When you get home I'll tell you all about everything," she added, beginning to smile.

"Think I'll make it?"

"Of course you'll make it," said Evelyn. "After what I told Mr. Bailey today."

"He thinks I did it," said Herb gloomily.

"Not really," said Evelyn. "Not now, anyway."

Just then another officer came into the room and up to the table. He spoke to the officer standing guard then addressed Herb. "You're free on bond," he said. "One of the members of your church came and bailed you out."

Herb stared at him in surprise. "One of my members!" he said. "Then they don't all think I did it?"

"No, of course not, silly," said Evelyn. She stood up, gladness welling within her. She almost ran around the table, and flung herself into Herb's arms.

# 9

T HE TELEPHONE call came on Saturday afternoon and
   Herb answered. "Tabor speaking," he said.

The caller was Arendson, the pastor from the Willow
City Baptist Church. "Remember I told you at the quarterly
meeting that we were going to finish off our new section and
because of that we had to install new carpeting?"

"Yes," said Herb. He could not summon up much
eagerness but he tried to put some enthusiasm into his voice.
Tired as he was, a trip to Willow City was not his idea of the
greatest way to spend the day, but the church could use the
carpeting. If the members still accepted him and he stayed on
it would be nice to have the newer material down the center
aisle of the sanctuary and over the pulpit area and the choir
loft, as the present carpeting was really worn.

"Well, we have quite a quantity of gold and it is in real
good shape. We would not have replaced it at this time at all
except for the fact that we wanted to match everything at
once."

"Gold will fit our color scheme quite well," agreed
Herb. "I'll have to get the consent or approval of the
deacons, of course. I can let you know tomorrow and then

drive up on Monday or Tuesday to get it. I can probably borrow a truck from one of the members.''

"Good. I'll wait for your call,'' said Arendson.

Sunday night after church Herb met with the deacons and they took up the matter of the carpeting. After some discussion it was decided to accept it, and to pay the Willow City Church a small courtesy sum.

Later, out in the lobby, Herb stood discussing the day's services and mentioned to some of the members that they were fortunate to obtain new carpeting from the Willow City Church.

"I'll go and pick it up tomorrow,'' he said.

Janet Vander Cook was enthusiastic. "It'll mean a real improvement in the sanctuary's appearance,'' she said. "I know I shouldn't pay attention to such things, but sometimes during the morning service I get to looking at that worn carpeting on the steps up to the choir loft and miss part of the sermon.''

The frank remark was so like her and so completely normal that Herb laughed the first really hearty laugh in weeks. "Now I've heard everything in the way of excuses,'' he said. "Maybe you won't have to listen to my sermons much longer.''

"Why?'' she asked in a startled voice.

"Well, not everyone is as completely trusting of me lately,'' he replied. He could feel soberness stealing over him again.

"Pastor,'' she said seriously, "I think a great many of our members trust you completely. Really. We weren't worried a bit about you. We love you and want you to stay.''

"That's right,'' echoed Mina Thorpe, who was also close by. "We need you very much, pastor.''

"Why, thank you!'' Herb answered and let his pleased surprise show in his voice.

"Them's my sentiments, too,'' said Ben Thorpe, coming up. "We need young preachers like you for our young people.''

Jim Carmichael gave Herb a darting glance and there

was a wicked flicker of eyelid in it. It had been reported to Herb much earlier that the Thorpes thought he was too young for the church.

Ernest Rhodes and his wife stepped up also. "We've been waiting to tell you," they said almost together. "We want you to stay. We need you and your dear wife."

"Dear wife is right," said Herb. "She's had some tough going lately. And more to come," he added.

"I'll be glad when *you* start preaching again," said Carl Johnson, coming up to take Herb's hand. "The supply is good, but I was really liking what you gave us from Ephesians."

"And *we* appreciate Ephesians, too," said Forrest Thompson, taking his hand. His handshake was somewhat limp, but Herb figured it was sincerely meant. They were all there, he thought, the church faithfuls, and his heart was warmed as he looked around.

"I'll try to get back into the pulpit again soon, but I'm kind of played out," he said.

"Great to have you with us," said the Joneses, coming up. "The young people really miss you when you're not here."

After a few more good-bys and well wishes from members of the church the Tabors retired to the parsonage, where Herb called Arendson, telling him of their decision.

\*       \*       \*

Late Monday morning Herb drove over to Carl Johnson's place to get his truck. Then he made the forty mile trip to Willow City, got the carpeting, chatted a while and had lunch with the pastor of that church. He got home around three-thirty in the afternoon and immediately began to unload the carpeting into the church basement. He called up Thompson to see if he wanted to come over and take a look at it. Thompson had volunteered to help install it.

Margaret Thompson's voice, when she answered the phone, was strained. "He isn't here right now," she said.

Some pastoral sixth sense alerted Herb immediately. "You mean — he's gone and you don't know where he is," he stated.

"Yes." It was a pathetic whisper.

Herb frowned. He looked at his watch. It was 4:00. The shift at Vander Cook's place let out at three, and it was only a fifteen minute drive out to the north side of Anchorville where the Thompsons lived.

"Maybe he's working overtime," he suggested.

"I already called."

That left silence on the line while Herb digested the fact that here was a woman worried enough to call her husband's place of work to check up on him, even though it must have hurt her pride.

"I'll be right over," he said. Without waiting for any more time than it took to get Evelyn and tell her he was leaving and why, he jumped into the truck and drove to the Thompson's place.

Margaret Thompson met him at the door with an anguished look on her face. She was pale and perspiring. "I just can't stand it anymore," she said. "I'll have to do something."

Even while she was speaking there was the sound of a car in the driveway and familiar navy blue Dodge Lancer drew up alongside the back porch.

Herb shot a keen look at his deacon. For the life of him, he could not fit into any evil kind of scheme, the man who fumblingly opened the car door and got out. Thompson caught hold of the edge of the door with one hand and drew himself erect. His gaze focused on them.

"Some . . . something wrong?" he inquired. It was evident by the nervous passing of his hand through his hair that their penetrating looks were disturbing him.

"Why are you so late?" Margaret Thompson's tone had a sharp edge to it.

"Am I late?" Forrest Thompson took his hand off the car door and pushed the door closed behind him. Then he started toward the steps. His walk was somewhat hesitating, yet he made no missteps, nor did he stumble. "Stopped in at the store for a soda. Must have stayed a while, I guess."

"Stop!" The cry came from his wife and it stopped him.

"What is the matter, Margaret?" he asked.

As Herb watched the little scene unfolding, he had an unreal feeling, as though the drama enacting itself before him was on television. This was not his sharp, capable deacon. This was not the man who, only last night, had reassured him he would be on hand to install the new carpeting. He felt it was his duty to intervene.

"Have you been feeling well, lately?" he asked Thompson, and watched him narrowly as he answered.

"Yes. I feel all right, I guess. Been a little tired. Can't seem to get enough sleep, lately."

"What I'm trying to say is," began Herb again, feeling desperately inadequate, "maybe you should get a good check-up. You . . . you haven't been to work all the time, you know. Where *have* you been?"

"Beg pardon?" Thompson's eyebrows climbed and he gave Herb stare for stare. "I don't know what you mean."

"You didn't report for work a few weeks ago," said Herb.

"Oh, yes . . . four weeks ago. That was the day the Ames girl was killed."

"Right," said Herb, watching Thompson. He could read nothing in the impassive face.

"I wasn't feeling well that day. Kind of sick to my stomach," said Thompson.

"Got the carpeting today from Willow City," said Herb. He waited to see if this rang a bell.

"Oh, yes. Gold you said, eh? Well, I'll help put it in any day you say," said Thompson. A bemused smile plucked at his face and pushed the folds into laughing marks. He was a handsome man, thought Herb, watching. His shock of white and black hair was still thick and healthy looking, not like that of some of the more balding members of his congregation. But there was a lurking expression in the eyes that Herb did not like, some way.

"I guess you don't need me, anymore, now that your man is safe home," he said to Mrs. Thompson. "I'll get along. It's suppertime and Evelyn will be waiting to hear."

He drove home and, telling Evelyn that he had a phone call to make, he went to the study and called the Bayview police department. He was immediately put in touch with Bailey. He told Bailey, reluctantly, what he knew about Thompson.

"I hope you realize I'm not trying to throw out a red herring for you," he said. "But I realize that I could be withholding evidence. And that I don't want to do."

"We'll check it out," was Bailey's noncommittal answer. He wasn't friendly; he wasn't unfriendly. It was like nothing. Herb felt a bitter taste in his mouth and remembered once again that he was not a free man, at all. He was a man facing a preliminary court hearing, a man who was out of jail on bond. He was not, therefore, really to be trusted. Who could blame the officer? He was only doing his job. Feeling a sense of helplessness and despondency, Herb retraced his steps to the kitchen. He sat down at the table where they were waiting for him to say grace. Feeling really humble, he bowed his head and thanked God for the food.

They ate, Evelyn tactfully refraining from asking him any questions while the children were at the table. When they were finished and gone, though, she asked, "Herb, dear, why do you suppose Thompson is acting so strangely?"

"What do you mean, strangely?" Herb had not betrayed Margaret Thompson's confidence so he wondered how Evelyn could know of any strange behavior.

"Why, everyone at church is talking about it. How he never seems to be paying much attention to what's going on. How he doesn't go to work some of the time."

"Oh." Herb surveyed his wife across the table and managed a wry grin: "I might have known."

He then told Evelyn what Margaret Thompson had told him. He also told her that he had reported the incidents to the police.

The telephone rang. Herb got up reluctantly and answered. It was Bailey. The man was more friendly, this time.

"Where did you say this guy Thompson lives?" he asked. Herb told him.

"Have you heard the news?"

"We haven't had our radio on," replied Herb. A premonition clove his tongue to the roof of his mouth and he couldn't get out another word.

"Another girl killed."

"No! No!" This time Herb found power to cry out. "It can't be."

"It doesn't exactly leave you in a very good position," said Bailey. "Would have been better for you if you had still been in jail."

"A girl from Anchorville?" Herb got out the question apprehensively.

"No . . . it's further away, this time. Willow City. But it looks like the work of the same killer. What did you say?"

The strangled sound that escaped Herb's throat did not sound human. For a full ten seconds he stared at the telephone in his hand. Such a feeling of evil presence struck him that again he could not speak. Could not think. He sensed Bailey was waiting. He finally managed to say, "Willow City? When . . . when did it happen . . . yesterday?"

"No, sometime today, probably between 12:00 noon and 1:00. What's the matter?"

"I was there today," said Herb. "I can't believe it. It can't be."

"Don't move," said Bailey. "I'm coming over."

Evelyn moved over to him as he put the telephone down, guessing from the conversation the gist of the news. "My poor darling," she said to him. Then they stood, looking at each other in a stricken silence. "What will happen now?" she whispered at last.

"God only knows," said Herb. He was not being irreverent; he was simply stating what he felt to be the truth.

In fifteen minutes there was a knock at the door, and Bailey strode in without waiting to be admitted. "What's this you say?'' He stood over Herb, hands on hips, glowering in genuine rage. ''Are you telling me that *you* were in Willow City today? This very afternoon?''

Herb nodded hopelessly. Evelyn had sat down at the table but now she arose and faced Bailey like a mother tiger defending her young. ''Why do you talk to Herb like that?'' she cried. ''He had a perfect right to be in Willow City today. He went on church business, to get some carpeting given to us by another church. He didn't do anything to slip his bail.''

''I hope you're right,'' said Bailey snappishly. ''Did you know there was another child killed today?''

''Yes,'' she said, but no further words came.

Then Bailey turned his attention again to Herb. ''This Thompson guy . . . how old is he; what's he like, and what does he do?''

They both tried to answer at once, until he quieted them by holding up his ham-like hand. ''*You* tell me,'' he said to Herb.

''He's one of my best deacons,'' said Herb. He began to talk, telling Bailey all the good things he could think of. ''I can't even think of anything bad about him,'' he said.

''That's quite often the case, of course,'' said Bailey. ''This kind of murderer is a schizophrenic type . . . two persons living in one. He is one person part time and someone else the rest of the time. To his world he usually is a nice guy, a fellow who is gentle and kind. Unfortunately, that is only a part of the picture.''

While the officer talked, something began to penetrate Herb's consciousness. ''You don't think I did it,'' he said.

Bailey looked at him quizzically. ''You're my big question mark,'' he replied. ''I don't think you would have pulled a murder in a place so obvious when everyone knew you were going to Willow City today. If you had been going to kill somebody, you'd have done it earlier, before you left, or after you got home, and used the Willow City trip for an alibi.''

''Those are the kindest words I've heard in many a

day," said Herb gratefully. A small feeling of satisfaction seeped through him.

"We'll check this guy Thompson," said Bailey. "Did he know you were going to Willow City today?"

"Oh, sure," said Herb. "I told him last night, because he said he would install the carpeting for us."

\* \* \*

In the hospital room where the elderly Mrs. Vogel was a patient, doctors were busy examining the now conscious woman. She was a docile patient, content to lie by the hour staring out the window, except when someone spoke to her directly. Then she would respond fairly well. There was one thing wrong, though; she could not remember what had happened on the day that she fell. Her world existed only for the present. The nurses would try once in a while to bring back that vacant memory of the past but with no success. She could remember her daughter, but often could not recall her name.

Today the doctors were taking tests to determine what, if any, permanent brain damage she had sustained. After some time they conferred and informed the daughter that her mother's memory was not likely to return immediately.

"It may be tomorrow, it may be three months from now," they said kindly, "but it will come back."

"That's good to know," said the daughter wistfully. "If only . . . if only there was something I could *do*."

\* \* \*

Wednesday came, with the preliminary hearing only three days away. Hanson, the lawyer who had been hired to defend Herb, had been there often and had gone over and over every detail that could possibly have any bearing on the case. Herb surprised himself. His interest in the outcome was so feeble it was almost disinterest. It was as though he had lost his grasp on everything that mattered to him. He was content to get up mornings, have simple devotions at the breakfast table with the family and then take a book or a magazine and read for a time. True, there were calls he had to make, and it was necessary for him to call the Thompsons to see how they were coming along. He learned that the police had taken Thompson to Bayview for questioning and that they had then recommended that he be checked over to determine if he was of stable mind. They had been unable to get any information out of him from all Margaret Thompson told Herb, and had finally turned him over to the Bayview General Hospital for a check-up.

Of course, Herb thought, it might be easy enough to prove that Thompson was a schizophrenic, or in some way mentally ill and therefore capable of murder, but not liable for his crimes. That seemed to be the popular trend today, he thought, to excuse everything a man did on the basis of illness. Actually, until a few weeks prior, Forrest Thompson had showed no signs at all of any illness. But that didn't matter either, Herb thought. Those kind of people were often "good citizens" living apparently blameless lives until apprehended. He would just have to wait and see what the reports were.

Hanson told Herb he could probably get the hearing set ahead so that it would be delayed until Thompson was determined guilty or not. But Herb would not hear of it. "I can't stand this anymore," he said. "I'm innocent and I want the world to know it. I don't want this to drag on. I've got to get out from under this pressure, this uncertainty so that I can have peace. I say let's have it and be done with it."

Hanson reluctantly agreed. So Wednesday passed and the prayer meeting was sparsely attended. Although the members had assured him of their loyalty and faith in him on Sunday night, they were scarce tonight, Herb thought as he looked around. Mrs. Thorpe and Dawna were there, the Carmichaels were there, the Rhodeses and Carl Johnson and a smattering of young people.

"What I wish," said Herb unsteadily to the faithful few, "is that we could just stay together and pray especially for the things that are troubling us . . . what I mean to say is . . . for me, and for this hearing that will be coming up on Friday, and for the Thompsons.''

The prayer meeting was tremendous, Herb thought later. Nearly everyone participated; even the young people seemed to sense the great need. For the first time in several weeks Herb retired with a sense of peace, so that he slept quietly and deeply the whole night.

\*　　\*　　\*

Thursday morning the telephone rang and Bailey's voice came through somewhat roughly. ''Had your man, Thompson, down at Bayview General,'' he said. ''He's a sick man. Know what they found? He has a brain tumor, and they are going to try and operate today, to remove it.''

''Then he is sort of eliminated as a suspect, isn't he?'' Herb felt a quick relief for Margaret Thompson who had been enduring agonies of mind for several weeks now, but realized that he was once more, as they say, ''the prime suspect.''

''Most likely,'' said Bailey. ''It leaves you in sort of a bad spot, doesn't it? Well, after the hearing tomorrow it will be determined whether or not you will have a trial, whether there is sufficient evidence to bind you over for trial.''

''I suppose I had better go and see Thompson,'' said Herb slowly. Then he added with a touch of irony, ''It might be the last time I'll be able to go.''

He made the trip in to Bayview Hospital to see Thompson, but found that the man was so heavily doped he was very foggy. He did give a few words of comfort to Margaret Thompson, who tearfully clung to his arm with the words, ''It's wonderful to know that he isn't what I feared, but oh, pastor, suppose he . . . suppose he . . . '' She broke down, unable to say the words. ''Just think of the ugly things I've thought of him these past few weeks and they weren't true at all. He's only my poor, darling Forrest, and now I may lose him entirely.''

''Try to trust God,'' Herb said, feeling like a hypocrite. He was no longer sure within himself that *he* was too trusting.

And he admitted to himself when he was alone that God seemed a long way off. Even the peace of the night before had fled off somewhere. He was, he thought, like a balloon, full of air one minute, deflated the next.

"I do trust Him," assured Margaret Thompson. "I know He cares."

Herb nodded. He knew it too — in his head. But it seemed a long way down, nowadays, from his head to his heart. His prayer before he left the bedside was brief. "Lord, have Your will and Your way in all our lives," he said. "We ask it all in the name of Christ, our Lord, and for His sake."

Margaret Thompson seemed satisfied. She squeezed his hand and thanked him. "I'll be praying for *you*, too," she told him.

On his way out of the hospital Herb decided to stop by and see Mrs. Vogel. He wondered if he would be welcome, if the daughter would remember him. It seemed a long time before that he had been there. He thought it would be the least he could do, to visit her, and he wondered if she had recovered enough yet to assist Bailey on his "case," as he called it.

Mrs. Vogel was conscious for the first time that he had seen her, and she gave him a slight smile when he introduced himself. He took her hand and told her, gently, who he was, and that he had been asked to come to see her, but that she had been unconscious when he came. "We prayed you would regain consciousness, and God answered that prayer," he said gladly.

"Why didn't you come back after that?" the old lady shot the question at him so fast that Herb was taken aback.

"Why . . . why . . . " he stammered, "I couldn't come, because. . . ." He paused. She wouldn't believe him, he thought.

"Because why?"

"Because I was in jail," he said.

"In *jail?*" the shocked old lady turned an incredulous gaze upon him. "What's a nice young man like you doing in jail?"

"Well," he said evasively, "There was someone killed, and some people thought I did it."

"Ridiculous," she snapped. "Absolutely ridiculous."

"I wasn't there long," he assured her. "Only a couple of days. One of my church members came and bailed me out."

"Smart man," she affirmed. Then she lay back against her pillow again. "Who was it got killed? How killed? You mean in a car accident?"

"No, it was a little girl, and she was murdered," said Herb.

"How murdered?"

"She was . . . was strangled," offered Herb hesitatingly. He was not happy with the conversation, tried to steer her away from it. This was certainly no matter for an old lady like Mrs. Vogel to be worrying about, ill as she had been.

She lay there eyeing him doubtfully, a faint frown between her keen old eyes. "You mean," she said finally, "a little girl was killed by a man? A sex criminal?"

"Yes," said Herb. He let it go at that, and then she seemed to lose interest in him. "I'm tired," she said. "Come back again, won't you?"

"I'll certainly try," said Herb. He left, and went home to spend the rest of the time remaining to him with his family, trying to prepare himself for the hearing the next day.

\*　　\*　　\*

Friday came in a sudden flurry of phone calls, hurried trips to the store, a conference with Hanson. Herb was not to drive to the hearing, he would be escorted there by Bailey and Hanson. Donn was to go to Mrs. Gale's and she had made arrangements to take him shopping in the afternoon. Pam was going to the Thorpes who were going to take the two girls horseback riding somewhere. Dawna had been excused from school and Pam was wild about going horseback riding. She didn't understand what was going on anyway, and Evelyn was thankful she didn't. Pam was too young, she thought, to bear any emotional scars from their present ordeal, and she was thankful for that also.

The hearing was set for 10:30 and Herb left with Hanson and Bailey at 9:30.

Several church members called after that, giving their assurances of prayer and warm words of comfort. It made Evelyn feel quite good. She suffered though for Herb, who, she knew, had already endured so much he was no longer the gay, tender, boyish husband she had known only a few weeks before. The pall which had hung over them for weeks now was destroying them, and so much depended on the hearing today. Their very lives depended on it. Evelyn wavered between moments of faith when she was sure that God had His hand on them and was protecting them, and fits of depression when she was sure He didn't care a thing about them. Maybe didn't even exist.

John and Ursula Ames, of course, would be present at the hearing. She knew they had assured Herb of that. They had seemed to grow wonderfully in the few weeks they had been Christians, and had seemed untouched by all the doubt and indecision of the past few weeks. Maybe it was because they hadn't been Christians very long, Evelyn decided. They were used to the ways of the world, and could understand sin. Evelyn wondered if any of the Christians she knew were capable of understanding anything about sin. They were such good people, good people so long now that they didn't even remember what it was like on the other side — the seamy side, as Herb was wont to call it.

Evelyn breathed hurried little prayers as she tried to collect her thoughts, and prepared to ride to the courthouse in Bayview with Anne Rhodes. She had become very close to Mrs. Rhodes since the night Herb was jailed, and she was thankful now that she had someone so close to lean on.

She hadn't wanted her own folks to come over. It would be too much of a strain for them, as her father's heart was not as strong as it might be these days. So she would have to get her strength from smiling at Herb once in a while to let him know she loved him and trusted him — and wasn't *that* a wonderful relief!

The Joneses called to tell her that they planned to come to the courthouse.

Mrs. Gale called to tell her that she was all ready to take Donn downtown for a shopping tour, and that she would be home with him later in the afternoon. She might go as far as Westview, she said, because there was a new shopping center opened that she hadn't seen, and her sister was going to go along.

Evelyn said fine. The time was getting short and she was anxious to get away. She hung up the telephone and it rang again, annoyingly.

When she picked up the receiver there was no one there. Or, rather, there was someone there, all right, but a voiceless someone, whose heavy breath was on the wire terrifyingly, noisily. Evelyn realized suddenly that she was probably only a telephone wire's length away from the murderer. She felt faint. As she stood holding her breath the receiver clicked down and the dial tone returned. She hung up, shaken, her hands unsteady, and went to get her purse and gloves, and to put on her scarf.

The telephone rang again. She let it ring the first time thinking, "It's him again and I can't stand it. I won't answer." But Herb had told her again somewhat sternly never to let the telephone ring as it could be an emergency. So she answered. Relief hit her as Mina Thorpe's voice broke on her ear.

"Listen. You won't mind, will you . . . I know it's too bad, but Dawna got a call to baby-sit and I'm not feeling well at all. One of my migraine headaches has come on. So I'm afraid the girls won't be able to go horseback riding after all. You won't mind, will you, if I send Pam back with Ben in a couple of hours? Can't she stay at the courthouse with you? Or maybe he can take her over to someone else's house."

Annoyed again, Evelyn said she supposed it was all right. She didn't want Pam at the courthouse — didn't think she could have her, in fact. But maybe they could make other arrangements later in the morning. Besides, she thought, she might be called to testify, or something.

"We'll keep her until noon or shortly thereafter," Mina said. "And then Ben can bring her over when he goes to work. He's working the afternoon and evening shift now."

"All right," agreed Evelyn, desperate to get away. She only wished Mina would hang up and leave her alone. She wanted to get down to the courthouse. She wanted to be there every minute possible . . . at least until Pam came. Maybe then they'd have to leave. She heard Anne Rhodes outside, honking the horn.

"I've got to run now," she said, and hung up.

*   *   *

At 10:30 the judge ascended to the bench and glanced over to where Hanson and Herb sat, to the left of him. The lawyer for the prosecution occupied a chair and desk, or table, actually, on the other side of the slightly raised platform.

"We are here today to call a preliminary hearing in the case of the State versus Herbert Tabor, accused slayer of Sally Ames. Do you have your witnesses ready, counselor?"

Hanson nodded in the affirmative. He had told Herb that there was one witness he would certainly like to have and could not have, but he did not say who it was. Herb knew he was disappointed that he was not able to produce her. Herb felt himself to be perspiring slightly and knew that he must be pale; his face felt cold.

He barely listened to Hanson's words as he replied. He might have given an outward appearance of calm but he was inwardly crushed. His whole spirit seemed to have broken. He would not have believed six months previously, that he could ever approach such a depth of depression as he now felt. The news that Thompson's problem was a brain tumor explained a lot of things to him, but left him still the only person suspect in the case, even though Bailey himself now admitted he did not think Herb had committed the murders.

Herb was relieved that his deacon was not the slayer. Next to going to jail himself, it would have been nearly as painful to see a supposedly fine person like Forrest Thompson be convicted of such a crime. A man like Thompson, he thought, was everything you hoped to have in a deacon if you were a pastor. *If* you were a pastor. He wondered glumly if he would ever be a pastor again. He wondered if he was fit to be a pastor. He glanced out into the courtroom and saw Evelyn and Anne Rhodes sitting in the front row.

Some of the others had come . . . the Joneses, the Carmichaels were there . . . but most of his members were on the job someplace. The Ameses were there sitting about halfway back. Herb wondered how it would be for them . . . the emotional impact, the agony of hearing all the descriptions of the murder.

"The State will attempt to prove first of all, that a murder has been committed, that the defendant had opportunity to commit the crime, and third that he had a motive for doing so. The State will attempt to show that this one Herbert Tabor, now serving as the pastor of the Grace Baptist Church in Anchorville did willfully slay by strangulation one Sally Ames.

"The purpose of this hearing today is to determine whether there is sufficient evidence to warrant a trial; to determine if a murder has indeed been committed, and if there is just cause to believe that Herbert Tabor is implicated in the crime."

Conrad, the State's attorney, called the coroner, Dr. Black, to the stand. "Did you examine the body of the deceased on the tenth day of September this year to determine cause of death?"

"I did," was the reply.

"What was your conclusion?"

"My conclusion was that Sally Ames, a ten-year-old white female had died by strangulation on or about 9:00 on the morning previous."

"At what time did you examine the body?"

"At 6:30 in the evening of the same day."

"And it was your conclusion that the girl had been dead about nine and one-half hours?"

"That is correct. According to my examination, she died at or about 9:00 in the morning on the tenth."

"You are positive about the time?"

"Yes, counselor, the tests were fairly positive. There might have been a few minutes either way, but we could say 9:00 for the purpose of the investigation."

Judge Klein addressed a question to the coroner. "Should there be a question of say, whether or not the defendant was not in the vicinity, or had an alibi for 9:00, then it could be stated positively that he could not have committed the crime?"

Dr. Black hesitated, his fleshy cheeks working in and out, in and out, like the bellows of an accordion. "I would say that 9:00 was the time of death, give or take a few minutes."

"Very well, we will accept your judgment as to the time," said Judge Klein.

"Next witness to be called?"

"Officer Charles Andrew Bailey, Lieutenant in the Homicide division," said the State's attorney.

Bailey came up and took the stand looking vastly uncomfortable. His florid face was even redder than usual and he ran a meaty finger around the collar of his shirt.

"Name?"

"Charles Andrew Bailey."

"Occupation?" the Counselor went on asking the preliminary questions just as though he had not already announced the man's name and occupation.

"What is your position in this case?"

"Investigating officer called to the scene at the time the body was found."

"Describe what you found."

"We found the fully-clad body of a white female about ten years lying near the lumber pile in the Standard Lumber Yard at the corner of Sixth and Ivy Drive in Bayview."

"Who reported finding the body?"

"A couple of school boys who were strolling through the lot on the way home after school."

"Did they report it immediately?"

"The call came into headquarters about 3:45 in the afternoon. I would say yes, immediately."

"What did you do then?"

"We immediately went out to the lot, saw the body and reported back to headquarters what we had found."

The questioning went on. Finally, apparently satisfied with what information he could get from Bailey for the time being, the attorney told him to stand down.

Bailey seemed a little excited and leaned over to whisper in Hanson's ear. The lawyer nodded.

Hanson turned and spoke to the judge. "Your honor," he said, "Officer Bailey requests permission to leave the courthouse for a short time. He has thought of something that may have a bearing on the case and wishes permission to carry out a brief investigation."

"Why did the officer not mention this before?" The judge turned a rather quizzical glance upon the two.

"The thought just came to me," said Bailey. He stared hard at the judge, who happened to be a good friend of his.

"It is a matter which has direct bearing on this hearing?"

"It does, your honor," said Bailey.

"Very well. Permission is granted for Officer Bailey to perform whatever errand it is he has in mind, provided he is back by 11:30."

*    *    *

Bailey left rapidly by the west door. He stood a moment out on the street, scratching his head gently behind his ear. Then he put in a call to Larson at the station.

"Make it over here on the double, will ya?" he asked. "It's important. And bring the key to the old lady Vogel's house that I left with you yesterday."

Five minutes later a police cruiser zoomed up to the curb

and Bailey climbed in with Larson. "Take me over to the Vogel house," he directed, "and don't lose time getting there. We only got until 11:30."

They entered the house three minutes later and Bailey went to the window where he picked up the potted ivy plant. He looked around. The musty room seemed strangely empty and waiting, as though it awaited the tread of an old lady who had carefully tended it for so many years. He found a small sack neatly folded up in one of the drawers and he placed the plant in the sack.

"What'er ya gonna do?" asked Larson mystified, as they left again rapidly.

"Go to the hospital to see Mrs. Vogel," said Bailey, nursing the sack with the plant tenderly against him.

"You don't get nowhere with her. We tried and tried."

"Maybe no," said Bailey noncommittally. "Maybe yes. We'll see. Something happened that morning you know, when she knocked this plant out of the window. I think she saw something. Maybe some little thing like this will wake her up."

They reached the hospital in a matter of a few minutes and went straight to Room 115 where Mrs. Vogel was usually lying in bed. The bed was empty; they looked around, surprised. Surely the old lady couldn't have been discharged — she wasn't that much better, thought Bailey. Then they saw her sitting in the small reception room along the hallway, looking out the window. She was looking flushed and excited, and the two men lost no time in rapidly closing the distance between them. She was in a wheelchair. Her daughter was in a chair beside the window also, and she greeted them.

"Mother is a little excited right now," she said. "It seems a little of her memory is returning. She just saw something outside that reminded her of something she had seen."

"That a fact" Bailey was keeping a sharp curb on the excitement that jumped in his heart. "What was that?"

"Oh, it was just a little thing," replied the daughter.

"Really. Only *anything* seems like such a lot, right now."

"Can you tell me about it?" asked Bailey. He sat beside the elderly lady on a couch.

"Oh, it wasn't much, I guess," said the Widow Vogel, "but I was sitting here looking down at the parking lot and I saw a little girl walking along with a red sweater. It recalled to my mind something I saw just before I got hurt, I guess, maybe."

Larson had not sat down. Now he bent over the widow, his lean face flushed with excitement. "I see," he said. "You saw a girl with a red sweater. When did you see this girl? What day? Could you possibly remember the day?"

Meanwhile Bailey had been clutching the bag containing the potted plant. He brought the plant out and held it up before her. "Remember this?"

"Certainly I remember it," she snapped. "That's my best ivy plant. Always had it sitting up in the window. Grows like a weed. Is it watered?"

"Yes, mother, I water it every few days," said the daughter. She was excited too but mystified by the attentiveness of the two officers. She had never been able to understand why they persisted in coming up to see her mother every few days. Now the area around them was fairly snapping with tension and her mother was looking as though she was just waking up out of a long sleep.

"It fell out of the window," Mrs. Vogel said, "and I had to pick it up and put it back. That's when I saw the little girl coming along the sidewalk. Pretty girl she was, too. I'll bet she'll have the boys' heads turning in a few years."

Bailey couldn't answer. A lump stood in his throat like a huge block and even though cops are supposed to be hardhearted he came near to kissing the little old lady. He restrained himself, however, and asked another question. "This was the morning you fell?"

"Yep," said Mrs. Vogel. "I remember it all now, clear as day. I had just had breakfast and washed up the dishes, then I went into the living room and pulled up the shades like I always do — for the day, you know. Well, I knocked this ivy out of the window sill.''

"Yes?" prompted Bailey as the widow's voice faded away a trifle.

"Well," said Mrs. Vogel, "of course I picked it up, you know, and put it back up in the window." She stopped and seemed lost in thought for a moment. "There was a car parked by the paint store, and it was kind of early, because the paint store doesn't open until 9:00."

Bailey and Larson looked at each other. "Br-rot-her," said Larson. "You lucky dog. You've done it."

"Maybe," said Bailey. He prodded a little further, scarcely daring to believe that the miracle had actually happened and that the widow had really recovered her memory.

"Yes . . ." went on Mrs. Vogel. "I remember perfectly. There was a man in the car and he kept looking at something in his rear-view window like he was waiting for someone."

"Then?" Bailey's voice was a little hoarse, but he didn't bother to clear his throat.

"Well, I was looking out of the window and I saw this little girl coming along the sidewalk in front of my house, and she had on a red sweater. Pretty girl she was, too.

"Well, the man moved his car and put it in the parking lot behind the paint store, you know, off the street. I saw him walking out to meet the girl and she kind of turned around and came back."

"What did she do?" asked Larson.

"She was smiling and talked to the man like she knew him real well," said Mrs. Vogel. "But then I saw them go up the drive to the parking lot and pretty soon he drove out and she was with him."

"Could you tell us anything about the car?"

The old lady sat for a minute then confessed, smiling a little, "Old ladies don't know much about cars, you know."

"Well, I know, but what I mean is," Bailey stuttered, "was it small? Dark? Bright colored? Can you possibly remember?"

"It was dark," she said. "Dark blue . . . no, maybe dark green. Maybe black. I really couldn't say. But say!" She suddenly seemed to realize what form the questions had taken. She looked up at them with snapping eyes. "Why are you asking me all these questions? What happened?"

Bailey tried to be gentle. "Well, ma'am," he said softly, "you were probably the last person except for the murderer to see that little girl alive."

"Oh!" The daughter suddenly put her hands up to her face. "Now I see . . . it's the Ames girl's case you are investigating. *My* mother saw Sally Ames before she was . . . killed?"

"I believe it," Bailey told her. "Sally Ames had dark hair and was supposedly walking along the Bay Highway toward her school. She was wearing a red sweater. We have reason to believe that the man who picked her up had a dark car of some kind. What we need now, Mrs. Ozswinski, is to get your mother released from here for an hour or so so that she can testify, tell this same story that she told me, on the witness stand."

"My mother — on the witness stand? Why, she's too old! They'd never believe her."

"Oh, yes they would," said Bailey. Jubilantly, he faced her. "With your permission, of course . . . the permission of the doctor in charge, I think we can take her out of here in an ambulance and have her at the courthouse in fifteen minutes. Then, she can tell her story and we'll bring her back, safe and snug. What do you say?"

"Why, why . . . I suppose . . . can I come, too?"

"Of course," said Bailey. He would have agreed to anything at all. "Who's her doctor?"

He first of all put through a call to the courthouse and talked with Hanson.

"I've a witness who will clear Tabor," he said.

"Boy!" said Hanson. "I sure hope so, because it doesn't look too good."

"I'm coming in in about twenty minutes with a star witness for the defense," said Bailey.

"Whoopee," shouted Hanson.

Bailey then got busy with the red tape connected with the release of a patient from the hospital. He had to talk vehemently and even a bit wildly to convince the doctor that Mrs. Vogel's memory had returned and that she was fit to give a testimony at the hearing. In a matter of minutes, Bailey was gathering up the loose ends for a temporary discharge of the patient.

"Never heard of anything like it," snapped the nurse who had to get Mrs. Vogel out of the hospital gown and into clothes more comfortable for the trip to the courtroom.

It was a real panic, thought Bailey.

# 10

T HE NEXT WITNESS for the defense will be called.''
  Hanson called his next witness, Janet Vander Cook,
who looked pale but determined, and who stated positively
that she had passed Herb on the morning of the tenth as she
was coming back from taking her husband to work at his
shop. She testified that she had waved at Herb, and that he
had tooted his horn back at her in a friendly greeting.

''Would you say that the defendant looked natural?''

''He looked like he always does . . . did,'' said Janet,
sliding a quick glance at Herb.

''You could not see anyone in his car?'' asked Hanson.

''No, he was alone.''

''Could there have been a child lying in the back seat of
the car, or even on the floor of the car when you passed him
without your having seen?''

Janet wrinkled her forehead in thought. ''No, I don't
think so,'' she replied. ''Of course we passed rather slowly,
as it was a corner, and you can sort of see into the back seat, at
least, when you pass.''

''Did you look?''

''No, not intentionally,'' she said. ''Still, I think if there had been anything . . . anyone in the back seat I would have noticed. Maybe you even sort of sense those things."

The State's attorney objected to this statement. "It doesn't matter what the witness *thinks* she would have seen," he said. "It's what she did or did not see that we are interested in."

"Objection sustained," said the judge. "The witness will tell what she saw or did not see and not what she thinks she might have seen."

Hanson looked at Janet with a smile. The courtroom had already heard, and the judge had heard.

"Thank you, that is all," said Hanson.

Herb was finally called to the stand. He summoned a reserve fortitude and tried to focus on Hanson in a way that would convince the judge and the spectators in the room of his honesty, integrity and sincerity.

"Your name?"

"Herbert Daniel Tabor," replied Herb automatically.

"You will please describe in detail your movements and actions on the morning of September 10th," said Hanson. "Tell us exactly what you did from the moment you left your home and describe everything concerning your contact with the deceased."

Poor little Sally, thought Herb. Now she was only "the deceased." He commenced a moment-by-moment account of his drive to Bayview and how he had picked up Sally Ames. Once again, now for a much larger audience, he recounted the words she had spoken to him, what he had said to her, how he had let her out at the corner of Sandhill Drive and the Bay Highway.

"Now there is some question in my mind," said Judge Klein looking at him keenly over his black, horn-rimmed glasses. "You say she made a statement about 'not being afraid anymore.' Do you think she had reason to fear someone, Mr. Tabor? Do you think this someone is the person who followed her, perhaps, and killed her? Is that what you are trying to make us believe?"

"I'm not trying to make you believe anything," said

Herb, stung momentarily by the judge's tone. "You asked me to recount her words and my words, and I told you what she said, and what I said."

Hanson was a bit more tactful. "I believe the question the judge has in mind is referring to the statement you made that, when she was riding with you, Sally said she 'used to be afraid, but now I'm not afraid anymore.' It is the question of the court that perhaps herein lies an answer to some questions. Can you be more explicit?"

Herb looked down the courtroom to where John and Ursula Ames sat, white-faced and fearful. He shook his head. "That's what she said, that's all," he said.

"It is the opinion of the court that the defendant is withholding something," remarked the judge sternly. "And it is the opinion of the court that, if he is to escape an unjust judgment, it would be better for the defendant if he tells everything he knows."

Herb squirmed uncomfortably before the gimlet eyes of the judge. "It is true that I am omitting something," he said slowly, "but that part I have omitted would only serve to harm someone and would do me no good."

"The defendant is refusing to answer the question?"

Herb looked pathetically at Hanson, who bent closer to him and Herb whispered, "It's the parents. They must not be hurt anymore."

A look of comprehension passed over Hanson's face as he turned to the judge. "I move the question be stricken, your honor," he said.

The judge eyed them sternly for a moment. The attorney stood, giving him eye for eye. "It is nothing that will help my client," he said, finally.

"Very well, let the question be stricken," said Judge Klein.

At that moment the doors were pushed open and Larson and Bailey came through them pushing the wheelchair containing Mrs. Vogel. There was a flurry of excitement in the courtroom, and the judge looked immensely interested.

"I will ask permission to call a surprise witness, your

honor,'' said Hanson, ''and hear the remainder of my client's testimony at a later time.''

''I would like to cross-examine — just a few questions,'' said the State's attorney.

''Oh, very well,'' said Hanson, ''if it is only a few.''

Herb was then submitted to a grueling few minutes of intensive questioning. Was he sure of the time? What time had he arrived at the Carmichaels'? When did he leave? Why had he not spoken of the meeting to his wife?

Then the attorney said, ''The two pieces of evidence which were picked from the lumber yard can now be brought for exhibit.''

Hanson agreed to this. Bailey and Larson produced the small white calling card and the flashlight, and these were first shown to the court then placed on the table.

''This is your flashlight?'' the attorney asked Herb.

''Yes,'' replied Herb. The knot in his stomach tightened again and he wondered for the dozenth time how his flashlight had ever come to be in the lumber yard, how it had ever come into the possession of the murderer.

''When did you last see it?'' The attorney eyed him keenly.

''I have thought and thought,'' said Herb, ''but I just can't recall the last time I used it.''

''The inference is that either you left it where it was found or else it was left there by the murderer after he used it on the deceased.''

Herb shuddered. That flashlight was, indeed, the crux of the whole matter, he thought. He had always carried it as a matter of course in the glove compartment of his car, and he could not at the moment recall having removed it for any reason. Obviously, either he had removed it and loaned it to someone, or someone had simply removed it from his car when he wasn't around. That would be a comparatively simple matter, of course, he thought. The car usually sat in the driveway beside the parsonage.

''The card which was found was also yours?''

''As I explained previously,'' said Herb, ''the cards

were passed out to various persons in the church at our calling program and could have been carried by most anyone. Or, it could have been received by someone in whose house we had called."

"Any further questions, counselor?" the judge asked the State's attorney.

"No, your honor."

"Then, if the next witness for the defense can be called."

"Now," said Hanson, turning to the woman in the wheelchair. "I will call our surprise witness to the stand, that is, if she can be brought to the stand. I had hoped this witness would be here today but it was not until this very morning that she recovered her memory which was lost due to a skull fracture incurred the day of the murder."

A ripple of excitement and a murmur swept over the courtroom. Everyone turned to look at the little old lady who was being wheeled up the slight rise to the stand. It was necessary for both Bailey and Larson to take the wheelchair and lift it onto the stand. Herb felt a thrill of anticipation — a quickening of his pulse. This was unexpected and welcome. But his amazement was great. The "surprise witness" was none other than his hospital patient, Mrs. Vogel. In swift comprehension he realized now that this was the "case" Bailey had slyly involved him in. She was to be, it seemed, his own surprise witness. Bailey then stopped for a whispered conference with Hanson who was nodding excitedly.

The hands of the clock now pointed to 11:30. Evelyn sat in the front row trying to catch Herb's eye, and alternately praying and mentally accusing the Thorpes for their slipshod ways. She would pray that Mina's headache would, somehow miraculously disappear so that she could keep Pam for the afternoon. Because, if they brought Pam down to the courthouse she would have to leave. This was no place for a child . . . she didn't think children were allowed. Her eyes rested lovingly and concernedly upon her husband, who sat now in the chair reserved for the defendant, chin on his hand, gazing fixedly at some distant point in the courtroom. She thought she should slip out a minute and call Mina and make sure of a place she could meet Pam when she came, if she had to leave. But she wanted to hear what the fragile-looking Mrs. Vogel had to say.

*     *     *

Mrs. Vogel looked fragile but, like so many of the members of the older and tougher generation, she seemed made out of raw steel; her recent wounds had healed and the rest she had had because of them had given her new strength. Once she realized what her mission was, that it was to help save the young preacher who had been so kind as to take time out to come and talk with an old lady whom he didn't even know, she would have sat on the witness stand until she dropped, if necessary.

"I have a witness here who will prove beyond a shadow of a doubt that, when Herbert Tabor says he let Sally Ames out of his car on the Bay Highway at Sandhill Drive, he is telling the truth. I have a witness who saw Sally Ames alive, walking south on Cranberry Drive, which is the Bay Highway in Bayview, on or about quarter to nine Monday morning, September tenth."

"Very well, I will accept this witness. Why is she being brought in here now, instead of earlier?"

"Your Honor, this lady sustained an injury on the morning of September tenth which apparently almost exactly coincides with the time of the murder. She has been unconscious until the past few days and her memory was impaired until this morning when she enjoyed what we would like to term a 'miraculous recovery.' "

"I see," said the judge somewhat drily. "Very well, proceed with the questioning."

Herb's reaction was one of renewed amazement. Could it be that God had, after all, intervened on his behalf and preserved a witness who could clear his name? Could it be then, that God was real after all and was actually going to move in this strange and unreal drama of their lives? His mind was busy with many things. He could not, for the life of him, imagine how his flashlight had gotten into anyone's car but his own. He thought back over the weeks, day by day, evening by evening. If he could only think when he had used it last. If he could only recall loaning it to someone. That must be it. Maybe he had loaned it to someone and he was mentally shutting it off so he would not have to admit the person's guilt. He barely heard the elderly widow as she told in a clear voice her story of the events of that September morning.

As he thought deeply, barely conscious of the words of the lawyers and the judge and the old lady, he was suddenly aware of a new consciousness . . . something that was filtering back into the fringes of his memory. There had been a night in the church parking lot that summer when one of the member's cars had broken down. Rhodes' car, it had been. Something had been wrong with the carburetor or something. And they hadn't had a flashlight.

Suddenly like a revelation Herb could hear his own voice, hear himself saying, "I'll get my flashlight out of the glove compartment. Just a minute." He remembered now. He had trotted over to his car, extracted the flashlight from the glove compartment and had handed the light to one of the men who was bent over the motor in Rhodes' car. To which one had he handed it? Who had been there, late after the service that night? He tried to bring back the picture of that night, the group around the car. It had all been perfectly normal. A normal group of people. There had been some kidding as is usual when someone's automobile stops running.

His thoughts were interrupted briefly as he saw a note being pushed into Hanson's hand. Hanson had finished with Mrs. Vogel and the State's attorney was trying to break down her testimony. Hanson read the note then showed it to Herb. The note simply read: "Herb: Mina Thorpe has a migraine and they can't keep Pam this afternoon. Ben will bring her here on his way to work so I'll have to leave." Herb frowned in annoyance. That meant that Evelyn couldn't stay.

He shot a look at his wife that said, "Don't leave me, darling, but I know you must." He managed a sickly smile. Some moments later, when it was ten minutes before twelve noon he saw her get up and leave quietly by the rear door.

The attorney was nearly through with Esther Vogel and Herb fell to his lone soliloquy again. Funny, he thought, how he could now recall when he handed his flashlight away, but he couldn't visualize those around the car. There had been Rhodes, of course — it was his car. And there had been Johnny James, a young fellow of uncertain mentality who was, nonetheless, a confessing Christian and a member of their church. There had been, he thought, closing his eyes, several persons — Thompson? He just couldn't recall. Then, he remembered one of the women saying, "Let Jim have a look at it; he can fix anything," and that would have been Jim Carmichael. But he couldn't recall having handed the flashlight to Carmichael. He thought Ben Thorpe had been there, and Sandy Jones' husband, Bob. It had been dark, though, one of those warm, sticky summer nights when you are too busy swatting insects to really concentrate on anything. He ran down the list again. Jim Carmichael, Ernest Rhodes, Bob Jones and Ben Thorpe, and Johnny James and himself. And one other?

Hanson noticed that he was far away and he leaned over to whisper, "It won't be long and they'll probably declare a recess until later this afternoon."

"I'm trying to remember something," Herb answered, "something I should have remembered before." He concentrated again.

Bailey had sent Mrs. Vogel back to the hospital with a couple of other officers and they were running down the evidence now, the State's man telling again of the finding of the body, the fact that Herb had seen her shortly before nine, the flashlight in the lumber yard and the little white calling card. In spite of Mrs. Vogel's evidence, it didn't sound good.

And suddenly, just like that, he had it. He remembered to whom he had given the flashlight to hold. And he remembered something else. He remembered that man saying something to him that indisputably made him the murderer, because he was the only one who could have uttered those words. The man had said, "Every time I think of that poor little kid lying there in all those weeds and dirt, it makes me sick." Who had told Ben Thorpe that Sally Ames was found lying in weeds and dirt? He himself hadn't known it and the only way Thorpe could have known it was that he had himself put her there, dumped her as he had dumped the flashlight out.

Herb saw it all now. He had met Thorpe at the post office the day the Kwekel girl was slain, so he had definitely been out and available at that time. The revelation made Herb want to shout, but it also made him ill. He realized now the strangeness of the man, a strangeness that one just becomes accustomed to and accepts. With the revelation, he reached out and took Hanson's arm.

"I've got it," he said softly. "I know who did it."

Hanson stared at him as though he had suddenly gone berserk.

"What do you mean, Tabor?" he asked incredulously. "Why? What evidence has been brought up that gives any indication at all?"

"None," said Herb. "Nevertheless, I know who it is."

"Are you sure?"

"Positive," said Herb. And he was. It all fitted so perfectly. Who had been there that Wednesday night with the whiny story of how bad things were getting today, and how he had lain awake nights worrying about his daughter? Who had held the flashlight, who had access to calling cards from the church? Who else had a job with time fluctuations as Ben Thorpe did, working as a delivery man for the Watson Distributing Company? He had perfect access to all parts of town at all times, knew where all the schools were. And Ben had been there the day Kathy Kwekel was killed . . . been at the post office, and had told Herb all about his ailments. He had looked rough, all right, Herb thought. And no wonder. One murder to his credit and getting ready to do another. And, Ben Thorpe had been in the vestibule of the church on Sunday night when Herb had told about going to Willow City for the carpeting on Monday, had thought if he went to Willow City it would implicate Herb even more.

What a beast! The duplicity of the man stunned Herb as he struggled to articulate as rapidly as possible to Hanson what he felt was the evidence.

Hanson's face underwent several changes as Herb talked. Surprise, unbelief and then agreement, as he nodded briefly and then excitedly, told Herb to just stay seated.

"Your honor," he said, standing to his feet. "Your honor, the defendant has recalled some things which have a definite bearing on the case, and which point out what we believe to be sufficient evidence to implicate another person for this crime. I realize this is highly unusual, but then, this has been a rather unusual case."

"The defendant is here this morning for the crime of the murder of Sally Ames. The purpose of this hearing is not to hear evidence that has no bearing on that particular part of the case."

"But, your honor," protested Hanson vigorously. "Surely if there is evidence that points to another person as being the guilty party, it would be foolish to continue this hearing."

"Are you sure, counselor, that you have evidence of such?"

"I believe it." Hanson was sweating now. His forehead glistened. "We have heard a witness who positively states she saw the deceased alive and walking past her house several minutes after our other witness saw Mr. Tabor turn the corner with an empty car. This should be enough evidence to point out that the defendant is not implicated in this particular crime in any way, and has been unjustly accused of the same."

"Hmmmmm." Judge Klein looked down long and hard at Herb, and then his glance moved over to rest upon Hanson, in an equally long appraisal. Then he glanced at the clock. It was 12:15.

"I think we will adjourn this session until 1:30, to allow

the counselor to gather together any possible information for a final briefing,'' he said. ''Court is adjourned. We will resume promptly at 1:30, one hour and fifteen minutes from now.''

Herb got to his feet. He felt no joy, with the discovery of the identity of the murderer, only a vast relief that now, perhaps, the world could forget Herbert Tabor and let him go back to doing the job he had been trying to do in the first place. He felt curiously deflated, unwilling to become excited, even thinking of what this would mean to the Thorpe family, to Dawna, who had just made a commitment to Christ. What it would mean to their church, now that they would know there had been truly an evil member in it. He glanced up and saw Evelyn coming through the back door with a puzzled expression on her face.

''Excuse me,'' he said to Hanson. ''My wife just came back in and she looks as though she wants something.''

They met halfway between the stand and the back of the courtroom. There were still plenty of people around, some of their church members present were standing to one side, probably intending to speak with them, Herb thought.

''Darling, I can't understand it,'' said Evelyn. ''You know Ben Thorpe was to bring Pammy down to the courthouse because they couldn't keep her there this afternoon.''

Hanson heard the words and stopped to listen.

Then it hit Herb. He could feel his face draining white as he stared at Evelyn. ''What did you say?'' he managed to ask.

''Herb, what's the matter? I told you — I gave you that note and told you the Thorpes were keeping Pam today. They were supposed to take the girls horseback riding. But Mina got a migraine, and Dawna went somewhere to babysit. So Ben was going to drop Pam off on his way to work. Mina said it would be around 12:00 because he had some deliveries to make at 12:30. But it's 12:35 now,'' she said, the words rushing out, piling one on another so rapidly they were barely distinguishable. ''Why, what's the matter? It *is* strange that he hasn't come, yet, but then, maybe something delayed him a little.''

"My God! My God!" Herb found his voice in a shout. It was a shout that turned all heads in the courtroom to them, to their spot on the floor. A dead silence fell as Herb reached out blindly and gripped Hanson's arm so that the other man winced. "We've got to find him!" he shouted. "Don't you understand? Can't you see? He's got my little girl! He's got Pam!"

"Who . . . why . . . what's wrong, Herb?" Evelyn was staring at him with eyes that looked through him, into him, beyond him. "What do you mean?"

Hanson was coming to life. "The murderer — the one who we think killed Sally Ames is Ben Thorpe. He was to bring your little girl to the courthouse?"

"Yes," said Evelyn, stark terror creeping into her voice and face. "You don't mean it . . . you can't mean it."

"What's going on here?" Larson had come up to them. "What's all the racket?"

Evelyn had flung herself into Herb's arms, and he found some solace in gripping her tightly. But the blood was pounding in his ears and terror such as he had never known gripped him, made him weak.

Hanson was nearly as excited as they, but he managed to articulate fairly well. "While the last minutes of the morning session were going on," he explained to the growing crowd about them, "Mr. Tabor recalled to whom he had given his flashlight some weeks before the Ames child was murdered. This recalled to his mind some things that that person had said to him which almost certainly make him the guilty person. But, in the course of things today, this very person was to have brought the Tabors' daughter Pam to the courthouse on his way to work . . . ."

"Just a minute!" A great shout went up from Larson. "Bring the cruiser around to the side door here on the double," he snapped to the young policeman at his elbow. "Call headquarters. They'll put out an alert to every police car in Bayview and to the sheriff's department in Anchor county to be on the watch for a dark car . . . what kind of car does Thorpe drive?"

Hanson looked at Herb. "A dark green Ford Ltd.," Herb said.

"What year?"

"About a seventy-four, I would say," replied Herb. He was held in a curious aura of unreality as he watched Bailey in the front turn and run out the door, saw other officers in the building running. Heard a siren wail on a cruiser.

"He was supposed to have brought her to me at the courthouse at 12:00," whispered Evelyn. Her lips were as white as the rest of her face and her eyes looked as though they had been ringed with blue-black chalk.

No sound, as all heads turned to the courthouse clock. Twelve-forty now. Thorpe was forty minutes overdue with Pam.

"Want to come?" asked Larson as he turned to Herb. "Or do you want to wait here?"

"We'll come!" said Herb. They half ran, half walked to the door and then they were outside and in the cruiser with Bailey behind the wheel.

The streets were lined with people, all staring. "What's up?" shouted one man who was standing with the crowd on the sidewalk nearest the cruiser. "A fire someplace?"

Bailey shook his head negatively as he rolled up the window.

"How can they ever find him?" asked Evelyn of Herb.

"By now we'll have so many cars cruising this county that a fly couldn't get away," said Bailey, overhearing her. "They've called out every cruiser in Bayview, Anchorville, Dudley and all state police cars, besides the sheriff's cars in both counties. The state police are taking the highways north and south, the sheriff's men are covering the county roads and the Bayview police are covering the city streets."

"He'll know," whispered Evelyn. "He's a monster. I *hate* him." Her hands were like claws on the seat before her. "He's so smart. He's so wicked. He's a devil!"

Herb stared at his wife in surprise. He had never in all their years of marriage heard Evelyn use such language or heard her speak so vehemently against anyone. He himself felt no particular hatred toward Thorpe, but then, he had no particularly intense feeling about anything — except his feeling for Pam. Little Pam with the short blonde curls, the small, pointed, innocent face with the blue eyes that looked at you so straight and inquiring that sometimes you wondered if she could see right through you. She looked, sometimes, he thought like the typical artist's sketch of an angel — minus wings, or course! The thought of angels brought to his mind that, according to his his teaching and his instruction, the guardian angels of God were to surround the Christian, were to protect and care for all those who trusted in Him. So far, they hadn't done a very good job on the Tabors, he thought whimsically, and then chided himself for the thought.

Evelyn said, "I don't think God cares about us at all, anymore, Herb. He couldn't. If anything happens to Pam . . . " She did not finish the sentence, but stared blindly out the window of the cruiser.

"I guess He cares, all right," said Herb, "but maybe we haven't been doing everything we could for Him. Maybe He is trying to tell us something."

"You mean — like Job?" Evelyn laughed and her laugh was as hard as peanut brittle.

Bailey turned around briefly to look at them both. "Why don't you pray?" he asked. "You prayed for everyone else."

Herb closed his eyes against the mocking look on the officer's face. He tried to pray; he really tried. "God . . . ." That was all that came to mind. Just "God . . . Jesus Christ . . . where are You?" If only his insides weren't so shaky and if only he could pull his thoughts together. He opened his eyes because he felt the cruiser turning a sharp corner. He saw they were down at the corner of town where the golf course was — the beautiful country club, where the greens glistened in the October sunlight like separate emeralds. The beauty was lost on Herb. To him, it was only one more barren area where there was no possibility of there being a car containing his Pam. His dear little Pam. He thought of the times when she had come to him and wanted him to read to her, and he had been too busy. Too busy studying. Oh, sure, he helped see her to bed on the nights he was home, and sometimes he heard her prayers. And once in a while the family went for a ride, or on a picnic, or shopping. But those times weren't frequent. A pastor didn't have much time for his own family, he thought in anguish. A pastor, apparently, was to have time only for other people's families — at their bedsides, at funeral parlors, occasionally at home. . . .

The police radio was crackling out sounds and Herb heard the report. "Dark green car containing man and a small girl sighted at corner of Sunnyfield and Tenth Avenue. Child wearing blue sweater and blue hair ribbon. About seven."

Like a whip, Bailey turned in the seat. "That your girl? How's she dressed today?"

Evelyn thought back wildly to the various strangenesses of the day . . . trying to act naturally getting breakfast as though this was any other day and knowing it wasn't . . . trying to get her husband ready to appear in court . . . trying to get Donn ready to go with Mrs. Gale . . . trying to get Pam ready to go horseback riding with the Thorpes . . . it all seemed so long ago and far away, not just this morning.

"I think I put a blue sweater on her," she said. "I'm sorry . . . I really can't remember."

Then, with clarity, she did remember. She remembered vividly putting Pam into a pair of plaid, bell-bottom pants, blue with red and gray, white, long-sleeved blouse, and the blue, cable-stitched sweater.

"Yes! That's Pammy!" she cried. "Does that mean . . . mean she's all right?"

"It means she's alive, anyway," said Bailey. "They haven't caught him . . . the car was spotted and lost."

"Mother verifies blue sweater. Probably the child we're looking for. Close in if you can," Bailey barked into the transmitter. It crackled back at him, the staccato intermittent and loud.

Evelyn prayed one small prayer. "Lord, You have to save Pammy. Please save Pammy," she said over and over. She turned and snuggled up to Herb, clutching him for warmth and assurance.

196

"Sunnyfield and Tenth — that's clear on the other side of town," Herb said to Bailey. "Are we going over?"

"You bet!" Bailey braked and swung the car around to head in a westerly direction. "We're on our way!"

The houses and commercial buildings, mixed in that particular section, began to flash by like pictures on a screen.

"What's that?" The words were out before Herb could stop them. He was trying to exert extreme control on himself, letting Bailey do the driving, trying not to make suggestions, not to interfere in any way at all. But, as they flashed past a schoolhouse on the west side of Bayview, as they were just breaking into the suburban area which soon would lead to Anchorville, Herb had thought he saw a dark green car parked in a school parking lot.

"What did ya see?" Bailey slowed the cruiser and looked at Herb in the rear-view mirror.

"I thought I saw a car . . . a dark green car . . . in that school parking lot," said Herb hesitantly.

Bailey braked immediately, throwing them up against the back of the seat. He swung the cruiser in a screaming arc and flashed back. They were just in time to see the dark green car pull out of the rear entrance to the parking lot and zoom into the one-way street heading north.

Herb took a good look at the car, squinting his eyes against the afternoon sun which was glinting in the windows.

"That's Thorpe!" he shouted. "That's his car. And Pam's with him!"

The next few moments were never quite clear in his mind afterward, as often as he tried to piece them together. Somehow, they reversed themselves again and shot after the fleeing car. Bailey had turned his siren on, and the car ahead of them now had accelerated to a frightening speed. Cars ahead of them and cars coming up to side streets braked to screeching halts as the siren blared around them, the cater-wauling screech echoing in the countryside into which they now were driving.

The car ahead was driven by a desperate man they knew, and it seemed as though he cared little for his own life or for the life of his passenger. They could see the child, first with face pressed against the window, just a glimpse of a white face with staring, shocked eyes, then they could see her burrow down into the seat.

Evelyn sobbed in sheer and utter terror. Herb shut his eyes momentarily, but opened them again almost immediately, because while he couldn't stand to watch, he couldn't stand not to.

"The fool. The crazy, mad fool," gritted Bailey between his teeth. A sheriff's cruiser had joined the chase and was following them close behind with siren screaming, so that it must be, Herb thought, the whole countryside, the whole world was filled with that terrible keening sound, rising and falling, rising and falling. The city police car had a yelping type siren and the sheriff's cruiser had a wailing type. The ensuing sound was indescribable.

*     *     *

Ben Thorpe knew the game was up. He had known it for an hour now. Some premonition had kept him quietly waiting along the curbs at various spots in the city, hoping that he could get away into the country . . . perhaps borrow another car . . . a lighter one. He was a fool he knew. He should have gone away today, let Mina take the child. The migraine was, he thought, just another subterfuge she had indulged in to escape her responsibilities. She had the headaches regularly.

The fact was that when he got up that morning he knew the day was going to bring evil. Evil rode with him and walked with him. He was aware of evil powers within himself and beyond himself. It had been a mistake to bring the Tabor child there, he thought, but then, how could Mina know that? It had touched off something inside him, some demon that seemed to be relentless and unrelenting. If only he had told Mina to bring the child back to the preacher's wife in the morning. But, he thought, that would have been too strange a request . . . if she had thought about it.

Now, here he was. The child in the seat beside him, cowering in terror, had not been placated by promises of an ice cream cone or a bag of popcorn. She had demanded to be taken to her mother. And the strange part of it was that Thorpe found he could not so much as touch the child. He could not even strike her. He wanted to, wanted to get his hands on her white throat. But it was as though an iron shield stood between them in the seat. It was frustrating and uncanny. They had started early enough, but he had digressed along the way, going down a couple of back roads so that Pam eyed him in wonder and informed him that that was not the way to the courthouse.

"My daddy showed me where it is," she said, eyeing him with a clear gaze. "I'll show you where it is, Mr. Thorpe, if you want me to."

"Never mind," he had growled at her and frowned so horribly that she had fallen silent awed by the strange new look upon his face.

And that was as far as it had gone. He had offered to buy her ice cream, and then popcorn and had been given only scornful looks. They had had lunch before they left, of course, Mina had seen to that, although he had been fidgety, wanting to be on his way. Of course, he had known he couldn't touch the preacher's kid . . . it would be death for him if he did. But still. . . . He had driven aimlessly then, knowing it was too late, that he was overdue with her, that he had no excuse for being overdue because the child would make him a liar, no matter what he said.

Yes, the game was up, and Ben Thorpe was a driven man. He no longer cared for the pursuing cars behind him because he did not intend to be caught. It would be better to be caught up in a single, blinding crash and go straight to hell than to sit in prison for the rest of his life in a living, earthly hell, knowing that his final end would be inevitably the same. Because he was not sorry. He was not one particle sorry for anything that had happened. He had discovered new powers and new sources within himself in the past few months and they had brought him momentary satisfactions. He hadn't had too much satisfaction for a long time before that. He had felt power and he had felt the victory of evil.

With all these things flashing in his mind he pressed a little harder on the accelerator. It was as though he had entered a new phase of reality and everything had become sharper, clearer. He could see the trees flashing by — the fences, the ditches, milkweed pods full blown with their gossamer threads; fall asters waving gently along the roadside and goldenrod dotting the fields here and there. They all stood out more clearly than he had ever seen them. Perhaps, he thought, because he was seeing them for the last time.

Ahead in a meadow about a half mile away he saw a giant oak. It was a thing of beauty, straight and tall, with full branches and leaves still green. It would, he thought, make a fitting death stake. He swung the steering wheel gently to the right.

\*        \*        \*

"What's he up to?" Larson's startled cry shocked them both into new awareness of the car ahead of them. They could feel their own police cruiser slowing down.

"Maybe he's stopping," offered Evelyn hopefully. It seemed to her that the agony could not go on any longer, that the sound had to stop . . . they had to stop . . . the world had to stop.

"The fool!" shouted Bailey. "He's going to . . . ."

"Kill himself!" said Herb. He did not recognize the sound of his own voice. "It's the only way out for him. He can't go back. And he's going to take Pam with him."

"No! No! No!" Evelyn's voice rose to a scream, and Herb turned with compassion and held her face against his shoulder.

The car ahead of them had veered to the right, first gently, then sharply, and the speed had not slackened. It was a dark green blur crashing down the incline of the road and then there was a searing sound as the automobile tore through a barbed wire fence that lined the roadside and hurtled like a bomb toward the huge oak tree standing in the field.

Then there was a confusion of sound, a terrible, rending crash, a scream. It looked as though the car had broken in half. Pieces of metal flew through the air, and a small body hurtled out, out and away from the car, to fall a hundred feet or so away.

Herb felt he could not look . . . but he had to look. He stared with straining eyes at the terrible scene. Then the cruiser ground to a halt and all four doors were open. ''Come on,'' said Larson, pulling at Herb's sleeve. ''The car may burn.''

Somehow they were all out of the cruiser and running. They found the place where the car had torn the fence down and went through, stepping carefully over the barbed wire that trailed on the ground. Somehow they reached the car but Herb and Evelyn ran further.

There she was, lying white and still in a crumpled heap. Evelyn tenderly reached out and pulled an arm straight. There was no resistance at all. Evelyn raised her and then laid her back and the child fell back into a flat position, eyes closed, face like marble and a thin trickle of red was coming down over her forehead.

''She looks so beautiful,'' said Evelyn, a great sob breaking in her throat. ''She looks like an angel. She always did look like an angel.''

''At least he didn't touch her,'' said Herb thankfully. They were both on their knees now and Evelyn's grief and terror found relief finally in tearing sobs that shook her from head to foot.

''I prayed that God would save her, but He didn't.'' The words came through her chattering teeth.

Herb put his hand on Pam's blond head, the shining head that he had loved to nestle against his heart. ''She was His. He only loaned her to us,'' he said. As he said the words, he became aware of a Presence, a Presence that was so strong he caught his breath with the wonder of it. He had often wondered what it was like to lose a loved one and feel the actual Presence of God lifting you up and beyond into that world of living that was unseeable. He was now feeling that very thing. For the first time in weeks he felt relief draining through him and felt the taste of salt on his lips.

"Here," said Bailey gruffly. He pushed them both aside, and felt Pam's pulse with his fingers. He then lifted the child's body and carried her out of their sight.

They then became aware of themselves and of each other. Evelyn reached out and tenderly touched Herb's cheek with her finger. "We had her for seven years," she said. "And they were good years."

The words wrenched into Herb's heart as nothing else had done. "I love you, Evelyn," he said, reaching for her blindly.

Behind them they heard a murmur of voices. "This one won't ever stand trial," said one voice. There was a reply that was indistinct.

Then a small voice said, "Mommy . . . daddy . . . where are you? Mommy? Daddy?"

# Epilogue

The Bay lay there, waters placid, a brown or gold leaf now and then going along before them. The dried reeds along the edge of the Bay stuck up like sharp swords along the water front. Along the edge of the drive countless millions of leaves lay piled, some moving gently with the breeze. Occasionally the wind would catch one and swirl it up into the air. Now and then a few late-hanging beech leaves would slip off into the air and drift down, swirling into the piles at their feet.

It was late October. Saturday afternoon. Across the thumb of the Bay a flock of geese came, honking and fussing as they hit the water and skidded to a floating stop, their voices excited and chatty, like those of old friends meeting for the first time in a long time.

Herb and Evelyn watched Donn and Pam as they trotted up and down the Bay shore scuffing in the hardened sand, picking up a leaf now and then or watching near shore for a possible frog or some other denizen of the water to appear.

Herb took in a deep breath, let it out again, sniffed the air. ''Someone's burning leaves down the road,'' he said.

''It's lovely,'' said Evelyn, ''simply lovely here. I wish we never had to leave.''

"It's been a real good stay here in this motel and get sort of put together again, hasn't it?" agreed Herb. He picked up a small stick and tossed it out into the water where it made a small splash. The children looked up and ran to them.

They sat, watching the two shining faces that leaned up against them, cheeks reddened, hair tousled.

"Precious," said Evelyn, reaching out for them both.

"Infinitely so," agreed Herb.

"What are you going to preach on, next Sunday?" asked Evelyn. The time had been a time of healing, but she wanted to hear the words, wanted to hear him say it . . . that he was going back . . . that he would preach. She waited.

Herb reached out and laid his hand on her head. It was almost like a blessing, she thought. Still, she waited.

"Well, I was preaching on Ephesians, you know," Herb said, reaching into his pocket from which he drew out a New Testament. "And I seem to recall that I was up to the eighth verse: 'Wherein he hath abounded toward us in all wisdom and prudence; Having made known unto us the mystery of his will, according to his good pleasure which he hath purposed in himself: That in the dispensation of the fulness of times he might gather together in one all things in Christ, both which are in heaven, and which are on earth; even in him: In whom also we have obtained an inheritance, being predestinated according to the purpose of him who worketh all things after the counsel of his own will: That we should be to the praise of his glory, who first trusted in Christ.' If I could get through those four verses, it ought to be all right."

"According to his good pleasure which he hath purposed in himself," said Evelyn. "That's what I don't understand."

"We don't have to understand it," said Herb. "All He asks us to do is love Him."

"You can't measure God with a yardstick," said Evelyn.

"But there's a verse in the Old Testament I'd rather preach on," went on Herb, "a verse that Dilson brought to my attention when he visited me in the jail. It means so much to me right now, and I'd like to share it with the rest of the congregation. Because, really, it sums it all up in a nutshell.''

"What's that?" Evelyn asked, interested instantly.

"It says: 'For there shall be no reward to the evil man; the candle of the wicked shall be put out.' ''

"Shall be put out," said Pam, blowing from her cheeks as though snuffing out a light.

"The candle of the wicked has been put out," said Evelyn.

Herb said with genuine compassion, "May God have mercy on his soul.''

# ZONDERVAN HEARTH BOOKS
Available from your Christian Bookseller